# MAD DASH

## WEST CREEK RANCH
### BOOK 1

## SAGE EVANS

**Publisher's Cataloging-in-Publication**

**(Provided by Cassidy Cataloguing Services, Inc.)**.

Names: Evans, Sage, author. Title: Mad Dash / Sage Evans.

Description:

Identifiers: Subjects:

First edition. | [Colorado] : Everaye Press, [2023] | Series: West Creek Ranch ; book 1.

ISBN: 979-8988328117 (paperback) | 979-8-9883281-0-0 (ebook)

LCSH: Ex-convicts--West (U.S.)--Fiction. | Siblings--Fiction. | Family secrets--Fiction. | Families--West (U.S.)--Fiction. | Small cities--West (U.S.)--Fiction. | Ranches--West (U.S.)--Fiction. | Cowboys--Fiction. | Western stories. | LCGFT: Romance fiction. | Western fiction.

Classification: LCC: PS3605.V3764 M33 2023 | DDC: 813/.6--dc23

*For small towns and those who love them. For all the hard times and revivals, the rodeo venues, washboard roads, and solitary trails. For my people, my best friends and twin flames, wherever you are. For my family, from big cities to tiny towns. For everyone I love and everyone who's ever loved me in return.*

*Truly this book is in memory of my Aunt Claudia. When confronted with the hardest things in life, she sang despite her pain. During some of my most challenging times, she was there, seeing things from my perspective, or attempting to. She was opinionated and strong and courageous. My life is better because of her generous spirit. I miss her every day.*

# CHAPTER 1

## CHRISTA

My grand plans meet their demise during an argument with an old lady over beef jerky.

Standing on the scarcely traveled side of a dirt rodeo arena surrounded by weathered wooden bleachers, a rusty pipe fence, flying flags, and a water truck making it smell like rain, I'm in misery over the only customer I've seen in two hours.

"But you've eaten ten samples so far," I say.

"I still don't like it." Mrs. Gentry's fingers wander over the sample platter. "It tastes funny."

I cringe as she touches each sample. She should be using tongs. Instead, she moves the shiny silver handles off to the side.

"How about I give you our special deal for preferred customers?" I force my most gracious smile. One thing I understand is being poor and proud, and while some people in Higgins, Wyoming, have enough butter for both sides of their bread, Mrs. Gentry isn't one of them. "You can have any flavor you want for four dollars." *Not that we'll make any money at that price.*

"It doesn't even taste good."

"But you're sneaking more samples."

Thick-boned and fussy, Mrs. Gentry looks up at me from the seat of her mobility scooter. "I am not!"

"In your bag!"

She purses her lips and puffs up her chest, sucking in air, about to launch a counteroffensive.

I suppress a groan. This is just another pothole on the road of a tough two days at the 100th Annual Whiskey Mile Frontier Days & Rodeo.

Calling me back from what a disaster my plans have become, Mrs. Gentry says, "I never take anything more than my due."

My pulse skyrockets until I hear it pounding in my ears.

I storm around the table to examine the bag hung around the handle of her scooter. She promptly accelerates to a new spot a few feet away.

I shout, "You thought I wasn't watching, and you were grabbing every flavor. Admit it."

Mrs. Gentry whirls, spearing me with a haughty glare. "Who are you, the jerky sheriff?"

"No. Yes!" I give up. Do I care? Yes, I do. Putting my hands on my hips, I embody the jerky sheriff, shouting, "Can't you see our booth isn't getting much business?"

With the way my temper's flared, it's good our booth is tucked in an out-of-the-way corner of the rodeo grounds, where no one visits. Maybe the loudspeaker blaring combined with people hooting and hollering muffled my fury. I glance back at Dad, finding him sleeping in the afternoon sun, reminding me why I'm here. The ill-tempered woman tormenting me probably lives on social security alone.

"Admit it was good," I demand, hoping positive feedback

will ease my wounded pride. "I'll send you home with all the other samples you touched."

Mrs. Gentry barks out a laugh. "Oh, Christa, aren't you precious." She speeds toward me and dumps the platter into her bag before taking off toward the other booths.

"Have a good day," I call after her, glancing at my watch. Then, for the first time since this fiasco started, I sink into a sling-back camping chair beside Dear Old Dad.

"Told you so," he says.

"Dad, I know." I can't stand listening to him boast, so I move away from our booth and stand with my back to the arena's fence.

It's almost the hottest part of the afternoon, summer air thick as fur oil, and I've got dust in my throat. I swipe a hand through my gummed-up hairdo and exhale through my teeth. I'm not too fond of the tight jeans, the cowgirl top, and how the outfit makes me feel like a wannabe. I should never have let my very well-meaning cousin, Skyler, give me a style makeover.

More importantly, I should have avoided that bet with Dad. I should have listened when he said this was a bad idea. We haven't even earned enough to cover the cost of showing up.

The first night was a learning curve, but by the end of Friday night, I thought things were looking up, peddling our jerky and pelts to cowboys, ranchers, and even a few of the newly moved-in homesteaders.

This morning, while I was processing hides through the tannery to keep our bills paid, I was primed for today's matinée and the closing night performances. The last day has drawn yet another sold-out crowd, admirable for a scorching Sunday in July, but the stream of visitors to our booth has dwindled, and of those who stopped, only two made a purchase.

The announcer's voice travels over a tinny PA system, "Ladies and gentlemen, help me welcome—returning after a few years of absences—the trick-riding Corbett brothers."

A gate clangs open, then hooves pound the arena. The crowd

erupts into whoops and shouts. I've known this show was coming since I read the rodeo program, and I refuse to turn around.

For every woman, there exists one man who is her kryptonite, and for me, that man is Carter Corbett, a cowboy who calls to mind how painfully awkward I was growing up. He was all I thought about from elementary school until high school graduation.

He's probably married by now. He might have kids. It's been six years since I left for college. I bet he hasn't thought about me since he wrote in my yearbook that we should keep in touch. Of course, neither of us did, even though he had written his phone number.

I turn around, and no wonder people are cheering.

Carter's riding Roman style atop a pair of stunning chestnut quarter horses. His feet are planted one in each saddle. His powerful thighs are flexed and move in motion with the rhythmic strides of the galloping horses. Trim hips give way to broad shoulders. When he gets close to my side of the arena, I feel a zap like he's seen me, but no, of course, it was only my imagination—a few stray fantasies combined with too many months alone.

Concentration lines his bearded face as he guides the beautiful geldings over a series of jumps. I grab the rail. God, what I'd do to make that man smile. *What wouldn't I do?* Trying to make my interest in Carter look casual, I let go of the rail and step back.

The crowd sends a new round of applause, and I avert my attention just long enough to watch Max, the younger Corbett brother, come out on foot. His muscular build and cowboy swagger are followed by a slim brown mare who walks along without reins or a saddle. When he turns and lifts his hands, the horse sits back on her haunches. *Like any woman in town would do if Max bothered to ask.*

That's how hot these brothers have always been—the kind of

attractive anyone can recognize, male or female—but they're not conceited. Carter was a lot nicer than most of the other guys our age.

My gaze drifts back to him. I'm turning into the same gawking teenager who sat with Skyler for hours fantasizing about what it would be like if we could marry those men. We would live in houses next door to each other on their massive ranch and raise beautiful families. We'd have adorable sons who could ride like the wind and crush their fathers' rodeo records.

The fantasies, coming from a girl like me, felt ridiculous.

"You're drooling." It's Skyler's voice near my ear. She somehow slipped away from her salon, probably to watch Max ride.

"So what?" I shrug, a little embarrassed at having been caught staring. Usually, I'd tune out whenever Skyler brings Carter up. The past belongs in the past.

Skyler's perfectly manicured fingers squeeze my shoulder, her blonde hair is exquisitely highlighted, and her snakeskin boots are dust-free, a truly miraculous feat given that we're at the rodeo.

I let Carter's magnetism draw me back to the show. Coming to stand entirely on one gelding, he hands the other horse to Max, who rides away, hanging sideways from the saddle. Carter cartwheels off the back of his ride, regains his seat, and gallops away. "Can you imagine how strong his abs are?" I let out a breathy sigh that makes Sky giggle.

The moment clarifies something I never realized as a teen. I pretended my feelings for Carter were a fluke because admitting I wanted something more than his looks and money would have required me to believe I was worthy of him. It's easier to see him as Skyler looks at Max—he's fun to admire but as unobtainable as the equestrian-themed Hermès bag she's lusting after. Window shopping never hurt anyone.

Behind me, someone says, "Can we get some beef jerky?"

I quickly turn and find a family looking at my table with no samples. It's easy to recognize them as new to the area because of their coordinating outfits and brand-name surfer sandals. Locals know this rodeo. Higgins doesn't attract tourists the way Jackson does. While I usually avoid homesteaders from the Corbett's program, I'm not about to lose a sale.

Dad's laughing eyes seem to bore into me as his smile grows. Smug. Gloating. If I lose this bet, I have to go on a date with Andrew Wagner, Dad's estimation of the best man for me in the county. He lives in a dilapidated trailer near the run-down trailer I share with Skyler. It might be convenient if sneaking out for vanilla sex was on my agenda. *But no . . . just no.*

Besides, Andrew and Skyler are friends. He's like a brother.

She snakes her fingers around my wrist and pulls me back. "It's not even halfway over."

"I'm not losing a sale because attractive men ride horses." I approach our display. So what if Carter's grandparents have been inviting homesteaders into the area to join their quasi-cult-like organization focused on "finding self-reliance"? It's not like I have to become best friends with them. Plus, their purchases could help us keep a few employees. Maybe if I get things running smoothly at the tannery, Dad can save enough to take it easy as he should. I plaster on my best fake smile. I suck at sales. "Are you all having a good day at the rodeo?"

"Yes," they say almost in unison. A little girl dressed in an outfit that matches her mother's cotton shirt and cargo shorts adds, "It's hot."

"You know how summertime is up here."

When they give me that squinty-eyed look, I don't ask if they just moved here. Instead, I offer them the real story of this part of the country. "It's beautiful, but it can be harsh."

I return to setting up the display, thinking of something more to say. The smell of sweaty horses, distant rain, cotton candy, and smoke from farmers burning ditches fills the air. Even though it sounds folksy, I offer some advice. "Hold on to the coolness of the night. Not everywhere gets that breath of relief, and by noon find a good patch of shade, or you'll be standing inside your own shadow daydreaming about a breeze."

"Or a building with air conditioning," the woman says, sweat beading her forehead. "What's winter like?"

Long. Windy. Bitterly cold. I glance down at the mangled appearance of my pinky, scarred by frostbite when I was a child, and when her gaze follows mine I tuck my hand in my pocket, but not before her eyes widen. She offers me a pitying smile.

People feeling sorry for me is another thing I can't stand. Maybe I learned that from Dad. Deflecting, I fetch drinks for them from our cooler.

The crowd whoops, and my patrons take their water to the fence. Skyler ushers me forward with both hands. "Get over here. They're switching horses."

I nod at my display.

"Go on," Dad says from behind me. "I'll take care of this."

"But our bet."

"Go." He rolls toward me in his wheelchair, every move of his arms making him grimace. "Have a little fun."

"Because I'm losing."

"Because you should have fun once a year, at least."

Such a smarty-pants, but I wouldn't change Dad for anything.

# CHAPTER 2

## CARTER

I LOVE this shit best of all: the effort, the power, the praise of a crowd. Trick riding is the whole package. It's strength and instinct and remembering I'm the man who set all the records. It's reviving Dad's brand of quarter horses and feeling alive after almost five years of numbness.

I slide down my gelding's flank and the crowd roars. Duke, being a showman of a horse and as well trained as he is, takes a bow. Then I bow, and holy fucking heaven, it's like the clock turned back and I never went to jail.

The announcer's voice booms, "How 'bout you tell Carter you want to see him again next year?"

A bigger roar comes from the crowd. Then they're chanting my name, and it's like being a victorious gladiator in the Colosseum.

Something akin to pride blooms, making my chest tight and warm. I've felt like the spurned son for so long that it's peculiar to realize some things from before haven't abandoned me. I stare at throngs of people all focused on me, entertained by me —loving me.

Without my permission, my gaze trails over the covered portion of the arena until it stops on my grandparents' box. They're focused on their newest homesteader's little kids. Oohing and aahing, and I imagine feeling disappointed over how Max and I turned out. They're not even watching.

My momentary high fades from the intensity of glory to a buzz, leaving me feeling spent like a fluorescent light tube right before it goes out.

"You're damned good at that." Max slaps me on the back hard enough to smart.

*Because I'm not good for much else.* The words sting more than the slap, and that's all it takes to set my teeth back on edge. Nothing I do will ever be as good as my little brother. The golden boy.

"Fuck you," I say, and the words hurt me inside.

"Yeah, fuck you, too." Max flashes a broad smile. He's a monument to remind people that optimists are everywhere. "We should do another rodeo soon."

"You don't have time for that, remember?"

"This is important. It's good for you."

I swivel on the heel of my boot and swing into the saddle. "Right. Of course, you're right."

"Carter, wait . . . We should . . ."

I should have let him go to jail like he should have, but no, I didn't do that. I kick Duke into a gallop and roar out the arena's open back gate to make room for the next show, but I'm going too fast, heading toward an unexpected blur of long blonde hair attached to a woman who darts out of the way just in time. Another one screams the shrillest sound I've heard in years.

I pull hard on the reins, trying desperately to stop or swerve. Duke rears back on his hind legs. His neck rounds as he paws the air. We lurch into a black and red booth and land hard, trampling a table, sending packages of beef jerky, totes, and furs flying. The hanging banner wraps around us until it rips free and then drops to the ground.

In front of me, a brunette bombshell has her arms crossed. Her dark, nearly black eyes are unmistakable. Heat blooms in my cheeks with a surge of shyness and nerves. Christa Blackburn still shakes me. Her father sits amid the mess in a wheelchair, stone-faced, possibly angry I've destroyed their booth but not yet raising a hand to do anything about it.

Sliding out of the saddle, I hand Duke off to a rodeo clown and focus on Christa. "Sorry, I didn't mean—"

"You weren't even looking where you were going." She pokes a wild finger at me, forcing me to step back. "You could have killed someone."

"I'm sorry. It was irresponsible. I shouldn't have been riding so fast."

"You ruined our booth." She closes her eyes and pushes on her temples. Her lip quivers, and her eyes pinch tighter.

Hell no. She is not going to cry because of me. I reach forward and grip her by the shoulders. Her eyes snap open, and I can't help but stare into the hottest glare I've ever encountered. She tries to step back, but I like how my fingers feel on her toned arms. I don't let her go.

I lower the timber of my voice. "I said I was sorry. I'll fix it."

She spears me with a look that could barbecue spare ribs. "You know what? Fuck the rodeo. This whole weekend is a disaster."

Her words feel like one more confirmation that I should have stayed home, and being the asshole I am, I voice my pathetic thought. "Because of me."

"You didn't single-handedly ruin my entire weekend."

"Then why do you want to fuck the rodeo?"

Behind us, her father laughs. When I was younger, he was the largest man I'd ever seen, with a bushy black beard and huge hands. I imagined him polishing his shotgun every night, his daughter the prize he'd die to defend. I meet his gaze and attempt to ask for help with my expression. *Please tell me how to fix this.*

She closes her eyes, and seeing the anguish in the set of her mouth, the lines around her eyes, I pull her toward me. She resists, and my blood runs cold. This woman skins animals for a living. She tans their hides in the most literal way imaginable, but she's hurting, and one thing I still know how to do is console a person when they're in pain. Lord knows I've had enough of my own.

"Hey, listen, it can't be that bad."

Duke lets out a high-pitched whinny. I can't see him from where I'm standing, so I turn to face the fence. He's fine, just gussying up to a mare.

She steps back until we're no longer touching. "You better take care of your horse before he tramples someone else's booth."

This is turning out to be fun. "Why's your booth way over here, anyway?"

"I don't want to talk about it." She tries to smile, and I give her one of my own, and she looks back at me with glassy eyes. "This is the handicap-accessible area. The organizers were trying to be thoughtful. You know?"

"Because . . ." Of course. Because her dad is in a wheelchair. "But it's not right you're way over here. You haven't gotten much business?"

She shrugs.

"You know what? We can turn that around right now." I pull out my phone and call Max.

As soon as the call connects, I start in, "Tell the announcer we're doing a whip show at the beef jerky booth in the west corner. And bring my whips and send somebody to look after Duke. He needs a rub down."

"Right now?" Little Brother sounds flustered.

"Now, Max." Fully confident he will do exactly as I've asked, I hang up without waiting for a confirmation. He owes me that much and more.

# CHAPTER 3

CHRISTA

CARTER SHOVES his phone back into the holster. "I need you to be my assistant."

"Your assistant?" He's out of his mind. *Why is he doing this?*

"That's what he said," Dad chimes in from the peanut gallery.

"You just have to stand still and look pretty." Carter smiles. He should come with a warning sign.

"What?" he asks. "You don't want to do this?"

I look at the lopsided table, ruined jerky, and banner he just destroyed.

"I'm good at this. You've seen our bullwhip show, right?" His eyebrows draw together in the middle.

"It's pretty spectacular." *And dangerous.* In high school, he snapped a lit cigarette out of Max's mouth from atop a horse at a gallop. "Had many accidents?"

"I can find someone else if you're worried."

"Maybe . . . ?" Of course, he's only doing this to make up for destroying our booth. Not because he feels anything for me. Only . . . something in how he's looking at me makes me think I don't know much about him at all. I thought he was probably married by now, but I peek at his left hand. No ring. I can't help but feel relieved.

Pushing the intruding thoughts out of my head, I recall the announcer's words about returning from a long absence and ask, "Did you stop riding for a while?"

"I was in jail."

*Who says that?* I half-laugh.

He flinches.

"Sorry, I didn't mean . . ." He must think I know all about it since Higgins is so small. I vaguely remember Skyler mentioning he got into trouble for fighting while I was in New York. Instead of following that conversational thread, I go for lighthearted and platonic. "I guess that explains why I haven't seen you around."

"Did you want to see me?" One corner of his mouth ticks up in a smug smile.

Warmth blooms in my belly at the way his pupils have blown wide. Curiosity. Attraction. Lust. A match to the mixture of emotions building inside me.

I am not over being around him.

"You haven't answered my question."

I lift one shoulder. "I guess."

"I like hearing that. Say it again."

It should annoy me, him telling me what to do, but having his attention focused on me, like my words matter, makes me a willing participant. "I wanted to see you."

His gaze is on my mouth as if daring me not to smile, but there's more than playfulness in his look.

"Let me take you to dinner."

Maybe it's the sweet tone of his voice, or maybe it's the hot tug of sexual attraction in my stomach, but he is having an effect on me that comes as a shock. How can he destroy my booth, tell me he went to jail, and ask me out in five minutes? And why am I even considering saying yes?

"Please, darlin'."

"I—" Did I forget how to talk? Or is this Mom's voice subconsciously screaming at me not to miss a once-in-a-lifetime opportunity? Her rant last night about taking life less seriously might be getting to me. I want to smile, but I didn't come home to get into a relationship. I should pack up and head to the tannery to put this disaster behind me.

Carter could distract me.

Too much.

# CHAPTER 4

## CARTER

I REMEMBER EVERYTHING ABOUT CHRISTA. In elementary school, Dad knew I had a thing for the girl dressed in buckskins for Halloween. He said she was a spitfire like Mom. In high school, she was intensely serious and even a little scary with her knowledge of skinning things, but she was also hot and confident, wearing silver fox mittens and boots during the winter. Most kids wouldn't have been seen dead in them, but she looked damned fine. Once, during junior year, she went to the lake wearing a fur bikini. Let's say it made an impression, but I remember most how she talked to me after my parents died. Most everybody asked how I felt, clearly feeling sorry for me. She talked to me about rodeo and where I might one day go if my dreams came true. I could tell she was trying to take my mind off what I had lost, and I appreciated her more than I knew how to say. Then she told me her plans to move to New York and seldom return to her hometown, which destroyed whatever fantasy was building in my seventeen-year-old mind. She always was too smart to stick around here—meant for big cities, big things.

But she's contemplating my dinner invitation when Max walks up.

"Where do you want this stuff?" he asks.

"Give me a minute." I keep my eyes on Christa.

I don't want her to slip away.

Max stands there holding the whip. He's screwing everything up. "Go check on Duke."

"You wanted your whip right now," Max says.

"Save yourself the embarrassment of having me kick your ass and go away."

Christa lets out an almost laugh, then presses her lips together and watches us, her look part amusement, part curiosity.

Max is my height and muscular, probably stronger than me, with a hotter temper, but he'll bend when it comes to a fight. It's no surprise when he walks off.

I refocus on her. "What do you think? Will you have dinner with me?" It's a question I couldn't ask back then, with her sights on leaving while I would always stay here.

Her brows draw together in the middle. "Um . . . I don't know. I would, but . . . Can I just put my booth back together?"

I hold my voice steady. "Decide if you're willing to be my assistant, okay?"

"Okay."

"It'll be easy if you trust me enough not to move."

"Otherwise, you'll find another girl." A little hurt comes with her frown.

Maybe dinner isn't a lost cause. "Max'll do it," I say, watching her start to smile. He'll hate it, but I don't care.

"I'll think about it."

I watch her walk away and start putting her booth back

together until it starts to feel morbid, like I'm longing for something else I'll never have. Then I grab the whip from where Max looped it over a hitching post. He's leading Duke toward the trailers. Christa's cousin is walking beside him. He must know I'm watching when they cross the thoroughfare because he turns back and glares at me. Little Brother has a two-track mind with an alternating focus on doing whatever I say and opening his restaurant.

Country music twangs from the speakers as the announcer builds up the crowd for the show. I couldn't get away with interrupting a rodeo anywhere but here. But Higgins is my home—a small town where families show up to watch the guys they know embarrass themselves mostly and occasionally wow them with something worth watching.

I grip the whip's handle, then, bending my elbow, I bring the thong up and down in a smooth motion until the popper splits the air with a clap and a quiver. Cracking a bullwhip is all about weight and leverage—a combination I mastered long ago. Unyielding precision is one more thing that makes me feel capable. Hopeful.

With my back to the arena, I glance up to see if Christa's noticed me. She's looking down. It seems she's about done fixing her display. I want to give her a reason to smile. While she didn't say yes to dinner, she didn't say no. Her body language said what her pretty mouth didn't. Maybe she'll reconsider. Or maybe I'm a glutton for punishment.

Her caution seems like one more way Max has life by the ass while I'm constantly dodging the horns. He's got her cousin following him around like she's a lost kitten. He won't give her a smile, while I have to work hard for every ounce of respect, every measly opportunity, every glimmer of pleasure.

*Crack.* My whip moves in a rhythm like a drummer's beat with an urgency that matches the torment inside me. The process is meditation. After a few minutes, I'm calm and ready to perform.

I coil the whip, then walk over to Christa. She hung the banner behind the rear window and used the tailgate as a table. Admiring her ingenuity, I reach for a sample of jerky from the platter.

"Use the tongs." She smacks my hand away, selects the piece, and holds it to me.

"Sure, darlin'." I take it from between the tongs.

The corner of her mouth lifts as she watches me chew the sample. I draw it out, chewing for an unnaturally long time, then try to keep a straight face when I say, "It tastes funny. You sure this isn't snake jerky?"

Her dad lets out a roar of laughter, and I let loose too, cracking up a little too much since it was a lame joke, but she has this effect on me. Loosening my knots.

"Snake?" Christa shakes her head in mock seriousness. "It's West Creek Ranch prime sirloin."

"It's good jerky. I like it." Using the tongs, I grab another piece, considering what it means that she bought our beef to make jerky but didn't call me.

A little huff of frustration comes through her nose. "Why are you doing this?"

I meet her dark eyes and am riveted by a strong pull of desire. "I can't tell all these people your jerky is the best jerky I ever had without tasting it."

Her brows draw together. "It doesn't taste funny, right? That's what you're saying?"

"It's delicious. In all seriousness, I wouldn't mess with you about your jerky."

She smiles.

I gaze at her long and serious, showing her I'm no longer a boy afraid to take chances, but a man with a past who would like to see her in his future. This pull between us feels good. I could be happy with a woman like her. Not to mention, bringing a responsible, down-to-earth woman around would please Pops and Nonna in a way Max isn't motivated to try.

"Let's do this," she finally says, and it sounds a little breathy. She might mean we should do more than sell jerky.

"Are you selling furs too?" I ask, seeing them for the first time now that she's resurrected her display.

"Yeah, everything here. Plus, we have more in totes that we can bring out if necessary."

"Okay. Should I get Max to be my assistant, or . . . ?"

"I'll do it."

"Good," I reply, and it's fucking fantastic. We take a few minutes to discuss the show order and go over each spot where I'll need her assistance. She seems a little nervous but is a fast learner, and after years of practice, I'm pretty good at this. She returns to her booth, and I step away to get started.

Just before I uncoil the whip, Max approaches. Christa's cousin is close behind.

He says, "If you're done with me, I've gotta get going."

"Stay."

He rubs the back of his neck and grimaces. "I've got a catering gig for the—"

"I don't care. Hang out."

"Goddammit. Why?"

"Just stick around with Christa's cousin." Even if I can't remember her name, I remember that she invited him to the Sadie Hawkins dance, and he wanted to say no but couldn't without being a dick.

Max opens his mouth to protest, but I turn to the crowd. Dads in Western duds and summer shorts hold kids on their shoulders, and moms are readying their phones for photos. I school my voice into one of authority. "Today's show is brought to you by B&L Fur Dressing. Introduce yourselves to Christa and her father, Leland, then help me properly welcome them by sampling the best beef jerky you'll ever taste."

A guy with a ponytail heads toward them, followed by a few other customers. Christa smiles in a way that makes this whip show feel more rewarding than anything I've done in years.

Starting with an easy trick, I move the whip in rhythm, pacing myself and warming up before I start. Then, improvising, I throw the apple I'd been saving for Duke in the air and snap it in two before it hits the ground.

Reserving half for Duke, I sacrifice the other half, repeating the process three times.

Next, it's Christa's turn to toss a soda can to me underhand. I delay moving as long as possible and watch her face as the anticipation grows. Then, I cut the can in two, ensuring the mess won't go toward her. We do a few more easy tricks.

The crowd lets out oohs and ahhs.

Reaching the end of what I'd planned, I send the whip out with a gentle touch, wrapping the slenderest part of the thong around her wrist tightly enough to tug her.

She walks toward me as I draw her in.

Once she's close, she unwraps the whip from her wrist and whispers in my ear, "I studied the bullwhip effect in economics class, but I liked this lesson a lot better."

"You'll have to tell me about it when I take you to dinner."

"In your dreams, Cowboy."

A mom beside us says, "They're so cute."

I grab Christa's hand. A buzzing awareness races up my arm as we take a bow.

Afterward, I whisper in her ear, "Those are all my tricks."

"I'm disappointed," she whispers, but there's a playfulness to her tone that sounds like innuendo.

"Did I finish too fast?"

She grins at me and shakes her head. Then she's looking past me back at her booth.

"That's it for today, folks." I close the show. "Don't forget to head for our booth."

She frowns, then smiles, then hurries away from me. Figuring Christa out is a little like traveling without a map, but helping folks I've known all my life buy things is second nature. I pile on their purchases, letting her ring them up until, about an hour later, we've sold all her jerky and most of the furs.

I'm so engrossed in working beside her that I don't notice the customer standing before me is Pops until he says, "Carter," in a tone that is none too pleased. "I heard you rode your horse into a booth."

Pops is a cowboy. One of the last real men. He's unrestrained yet incredibly successful. Not to mention wealthy. I swear he could kill with a look.

"I . . . Uh . . . Yes, sir. That's right." I stumble over my words like I'm still scared of him, which I am, but I swear it's not genuine fear. It's only that he's holding all my dreams in his spare pocket. I'd give anything to keep Dad's legacy alive, including kissing this old man's ass.

He's staring at me and frowning with his eyes narrowed. He expects me to let him down, but he still doesn't like this latest disappointment. "Your grandmother doesn't need you embarrassing her. You hear me, boy?"

"Yes, sir."

"He's been great." Christa puts her hand on my shoulder, sending a wave of heat through me. "It wasn't his fault."

She smiles at Pops. If anyone can melt his frigid heart, it would be a beautiful woman like her.

I recover my composure. "Pops, you remember Christa Blackburn and her father, Leland? This is their booth."

Leland rolls toward us in his wheelchair and extends a hand. "It's great to see you again, Charles."

Pops's demeanor finally softens into an almost smile. He gives Leland's hand a shake. "Janet and I were sorry to hear about your MS. How are you holding up?"

"Well as can be expected. Christa's come from New York to help at the tannery. Having her home has been a bright spot."

"I've been hoping to have you taxidermy the bear I plan to shoot this season."

"We're up for it," Leland says. "Come on by when you're ready."

"I'll do that." Pops turns on me. "Get back to the ranch."

"Yes, sir." I swear I don't need a brain when I'm around him. I try to quell my anger and embarrassment, but before I do, Christa and Leland shift to focus on their display. Pops returns to Nonna's side. She's cooing over a baby boy. I stare for too long, wanting to claim that child as my own. To have Nonna's attention focused on me. To know the future of the ranch is secured by my offspring. I suck in a breath through clenched teeth. Goddammit. If I want a son, I need a wife. I needed one nine months ago.

"Hey, are you okay?" Christa says near my ear.

"Yeah. I'll help you pack up."

"Thanks to you, there's not much left. We can get it. Besides it sounds like you need to get back."

"What about dinner?" I say it like it's my only hope. Maybe it is.

"I have a boyfriend."

"No, she doesn't," her father calls behind us. "She's just stubborn."

"I do too." She blushes scarlet.

There's more love than mirth in her father's expression. "Who?"

"Uh . . . Andrew?"

"Do you want to call Andrew right now?" her father asks.

Father and daughter exchange a lethal look.

It's a little humiliating that she's lied to avoid me. Hearing her father say she returned to help them explains why the tannery's success seems essential to her. Will she stick around for good?

I pick up one of their brochures. Their services include blade sharpening, machine repair, and sales, wet tanning, dry tanking, fleshing and salting hides, and taxidermy. I'm getting desperate for ideas when I flip the page to their nuisance wildlife trapping service. We've got endless problems with beavers. We won't have to pull out the dams if we hire someone to trap the beavers before they build them. It feels good to consider how I would run things if I had some authority over my family's ranch.

"How do you handle nuisance trapping for beavers?" I ask.

Leland says, "You should see my girl set a suitcase trap. Isn't that right, Christa?"

She sends her dad a stink eye, then turns to me flatly. "What's the problem?"

"Beavers all over the ranch. It sounds like you're just what we need. When can you come out?" I wait, hopeful as a kid on Christmas.

"How about tomorrow afternoon?" Leland says.

"Let me check our schedule." Christa gives her father one more chilling look.

And it seems she's still the hot but scary girl I wanted to date but never asked out.

This may be my new favorite pastime, as complicated as calculus and requiring more finesse than trick-riding.

# CHAPTER 5



## CHRISTA

Driving toward the hospital on my way to Dad's appointment, a day after Carter invited me to dinner, I still tell myself that turning him down was the only choice. I'm here to focus on Dad's health and the tannery. That's it. I'm not looking for romance.

Carter's not the kind of guy that I could go out with one time and forget about. He would be a major distraction. But I keep thinking about how he looked at me when he said, *Please, darlin'*. He stuck around and helped us at the rodeo even though he didn't have to.

Maybe there's a chance for something more between us. I was wrong to assume he was married. What else am I wrong about?

It's been ages since I've felt this interested in a guy.

My subconscious wants what it wants. It doesn't care that I

have no time to date or that Carter would most likely move on and leave me wanting more. Like that day at the lake junior year when he got a call from Mandy Morgan, much prettier and more popular than me, and left me embarrassed for believing he wanted to be more than my friend.

Not that old memories matter, but Carter's not the kind of man I can fall for just because he rode his horse into my booth at the rodeo, not unless I want to mess everything up.

We're on the verge of losing everything Dad has worked for, and Mom's drinking is worse than ever.

I park and walk toward the Corbett Wing of the Pultney County Regional Hospital. Dad refused to let me drive him. He doesn't want me here. So what? I'm tired of being kept in the dark about his illness. I want answers and advice about how I can help him get better.

That's why I'm back home.

After this is sorted, I'll go back to New York, or somewhere.

The hospital's automatic entry doors swoosh open. A blast of cold air hits my hot skin with an arid contrast to the afternoon heat. Dad's insistence that I shouldn't come washes over me with icy foreboding caused by more than the sweat on my shirt.

I ride the elevator to the neurology department's modern lobby, with muted carpet and pastel paintings.

Dad's steady gaze hits me. "We talked about this, Christa. I don't want you here."

I pop into the chair beside his wheelchair as if his insistence on keeping me out isn't a wound. "I'd rather be anywhere else on the planet. You know that's true." When he doesn't respond, I put my hand on his knee. "I wish you weren't sick, but wishing won't help me get what I want. Isn't that what you used to tell me?"

"This isn't about getting into college."

"I know you don't want me in the room with the doctor. I understand, but Dad, please, I need to know how I can help you."

"Don't make me grumpy." He plays his signature line, which even now has me offering him a tight smile, because Dad is one of the most patient, enduring people I know.

"I'm not trying to. I want to hear what the doctor says. Can't you understand?"

"I understand, but I told you not to come."

"I'm stuck then, aren't I? I'm just going to worry with no basis to do anything—"

"Let's talk about when you're going to go on that long-promised date with Andrew." In a trademark move, Dad has swiftly reasserted control over the conversation.

"I don't want to talk about that."

"Well, then, we're at an impasse."

"Why insist on forcing me to date?"

"Why insist on coming to the doctor when I've asked you not to?"

"Because I care."

"Says Pot to Kettle." Dad fixes me with a determined stare. His eyes are so dark, it's like looking into the space between the stars.

"I know you care, and I'll go on a date with Andrew. I promise. As soon as you let me talk to the doctor."

Dad offers me the tiniest smile, then persists in his infuriating stall tactic. "What's this with refusing Carter? You like him, right?"

He's a master at evasion, too good for me to overcome because he knows me so well, and I'm so busy trying to keep him from seeing through my excuses that I can't respond. Of course, he remembers I had a crush on Carter in school. But that was a long, long time ago. I don't even know him anymore.

"I'm not insisting you date Carter or Andrew," Dad says, "but at least admit you're unhappy."

"I'm thrilled to be home."

"I was so proud of you."

Dad did everything he could to support me, helping me

choose colleges and encouraging me to leave when I would have been too scared to go—even though having me gone made things harder for him and Mom. He was proud of me when I got a rowing scholarship, and he wants me to use my education, but what better way is there for me to use it than being here with him while saving his business? Spending time with him while he's sick is precisely the right thing for me to do.

"Leland Blackburn," a chipper nurse calls from near the door.

"You wait out here." Dad's strong arms are no longer equally muscular, and he struggles to wheel himself in a straight line. I get up to push him, and he gives me a look I know all too well.

I plop back down. He can barely get around on his own. I've read what the internet says about multiple sclerosis, and it's scary.

Dad accepts help from the nurse, and they disappear behind the office walls.

Feeling stuck and wanting to make the best of things by not causing a scene or making myself a nuisance, I pull out my phone and browse social media. One of my former teammates is an Olympic prospect. As much as I once thought I could do big things, I wasn't dedicated enough to be an Olympian. I'm not even sure why I care about that anymore. I'm not sure what I care about except being here with Dad, making sure he and Mom are okay.

Still worried about Dad's appointment, I shift to read about MS again, but I've already read countless articles. I tuck my phone into my purse. I should be at the tannery, catching up on our late deliveries. Customers have waited for months. I should be doing something meaningful, but is that my future? Processing animal skin?

My leg jiggles with the need to act. I need to move, but I want to catch Dad when he comes out.

I walk into the hall for a minute to breathe. But I walk and walk. I'm still looking for a suitable distraction when I reach the cafeteria on the lower level. I read the flyers on a tackboard.

R&S Ammo is helping Make-A-Wish send a kid to a Bronco game. I've always believed in taking a "help others, help yourself" approach to life. Especially now, with Dad sick, it makes sense.

I retrace my path. A boy with a cowboy hat, boots, and a smile a mile wide comes skipping down the hall with his mom trailing behind. She shares his coloring, but her face is haunted by gaunt cheeks and that singular air of desperation unique to a parent when their child's very sick. They're a bittersweet-looking pair, reminding me of that Make-A-Wish flier, but his contrasting "I Love NY" T-shirt is what grabs me.

Maybe he had a wish trip and went to New York. Maybe he's like me, growing up here and dreaming of someday moving to New York. Perhaps it's his wish advertised on the flyer. But no, that was for a Broncos game.

"Mom, can I get a Coke and a burrito?" the boy asks.

"I thought you wanted that new roping dummy."

"I know, but I'm hungry. We've been here since dark, and I don't want more sandwiches."

"We can't afford to eat here and save for your roping dummy."

"But, Mom, that guy bought your lunch yesterday. You're supposed to pay it forward, like that movie."

"Nice try, Jake, but buying food for ourselves isn't the same as giving to someone else."

"Can we buy her some lunch?" The boy points at me.

"That's the right spirit, at least." She brushes a hand over his back, then offers me an embarrassed smile and says in a tight voice, "Someone bought my lunch at work yesterday, and we watched *Pay It Forward* last night. You know that movie about the boy who has a class project to make the world a better place?"

"I love that movie," I reply.

"Can we buy you something to do our part?" she asks.

"It's so sweet of you, but . . . I don't know. I need to—"

"Please," the boy says, drawing out the word. "We want to, and I'm hungry."

"It's fine," she says. "We want to."

Of course I agree because it seems the mom is on board, and apparently a cute smile is all it takes to wrap me around a child's finger. I'll have to remember that in case I'm ever a mother.

Once they're in line to get food, I learn he's seven-year-old Jake Foster, and his mom is Emily. I'm pretty sure we went to high school together, but she was a few years older, and we never knew each other. I ask Jake if he's been to New York.

"No." His forehead crinkles.

"Your shirt, silly," Emily says to him. Then she says, "He likes it because it's soft."

"Oh, cool." Jake's disinterest in New York may have saved me from saying too much about why I went away and subsequently decided being here was better.

Once Jake has his burrito and I've gotten a cup of coffee and convinced Emily to get one too, I offer to pay, but she deflects. "If you want to stay, we could use the company."

"It gets lonely here, doesn't it?" I ask because I feel it too—the weight of knowing someone you love is ill. When she nods, I volunteer a little of my story, hoping it will make her more comfortable. "My dad is upstairs. He has MS."

"That must be rough."

"Yeah," I reply, "it is."

"Jake has leukemia. We're waiting to see how his latest tests come back."

"We practically live here," Jake says. Up close, he has an adorable smattering of freckles across his nose and cheeks that match his mom's.

I ask him, "What do you like to do for fun?"

"I watch cowboy movies and rodeo and practice with my rope."

"You rope while watching TV?"

"Jake isn't allowed to rope inside," his mom says to me, then asks him, "Are you?"

"I would if Mom would let me." Jake grins.

"Did you go to the rodeo?" I ask.

"We were late," Jake says.

"I had to work," Emily adds with a hint of defensiveness.

"I wish I could be a cowboy." Jake's voice is quiet and earnest.

Reading about Make-A-Wish, participating in a *Pay It Forward*-inspired act of kindness, and having a sick boy make a simple wish, it feels like the finger of God is moving pieces on a chess board. The combined events can't be interpreted as anything other than fate.

I sip my coffee. Without spending much, I can help Jake be a cowboy—if only for a day. Maybe make his life just a little better. A warm glow comes over me. I want to offer but need to check with Emily first, so I ask her for a moment alone.

She raises her eyebrows, then asks, "Jakey, will you take our trash?"

Once he's out of earshot, I ask, "Would it be okay if I help Jake be a cowboy for a day?"

Emily tilts her head.

I hurry to add, "I have a friend with a small pasture, a few horses, and a roping dummy. My family can put together a cowboy outfit."

Emily's eyes are wet, and Jake is back.

"Christa wants to make your dream come true," she says, then clears her throat. "She's going to help you be a real cowboy."

"You are?" His voice holds adorable incredulity.

"Just for a day." Hoping not to oversell my abilities, I add, "We'll do everything we can to make it a genuine Western experience."

"I want to be like the Corbett brothers," Jake says.

*Of course he does.* "They're pretty cool, aren't they?"

"You know them?" he asks like they're movie stars.

"I do." My voice sounds different, tight, and uncertain. Should I ask Carter to help? He already supported us at the rodeo.

"Will they come?" Jake asks.

I hesitate. I could ask Max instead of Carter?

Emily says, "Whatever you have planned will be amazing."

"I want to meet the Corbett brothers," Jake says, earning himself a mom look.

If I ask, will Carter agree? He did leave his phone number with Dad "in case our schedule worked." Engaging in self-sabotage, I snuck the card he wrote on from Dad's stack and slipped it into my pocket, promising I'd never call him.

As I look across the table, I don't think there are words to describe the eager look of excitement and joy on Jake's face.

I could give him his real dream, but calling Carter after I rejected him and then asking for a favor . . . My nerves buzz.

# CHAPTER 6

## CARTER

A BEAUTIFUL BUCKSKIN mare trots around our big arena. She's well-balanced and has good bone alignment and clean movements. Her light mane and tail are glossy enough to shine in the afternoon sun. With her lineage, she'd do well in our breeding program.

I slide onto a bench and strip off my collared shirt, leaving my sweat-soaked t-shirt on because Pops is here, and he'd disapprove of me taking it off. Maybe that's because he doesn't approve of anything I do. Or maybe, I'm just annoyed because he's over there talking to Davis, our farm foreman when I'm the one who asked the seller to bring the mare. I want Pops's ear about our plans.

I try to shake off my frustration. Soon enough, I'll prove myself, but it still feels hopeless.

*I could quit trying* because only a fool would repeat the same approach and expect a new outcome. But I can't give up on Dad's breeding program. Without it, I feel dead inside, worse than in jail.

When the handler stops, the mare stands so still. It's like she's as charmed by me as I am by her.

I walk toward Pops and offer to lunge her.

"Attitude has a lot to do with how a man handles a horse," Pops says as if I don't already know. It's not like he's unaware I've been working with horses my entire life, but he must lecture.

This bizarre form of interaction is our normal state. "You can't fight a horse if you want the best out of them."

Davis smirks. I want to punch him in the neck but try to keep my temper. Even when I'm frustrated, I hold my voice low and even.

I take Pops's grunt as permission. I've known the woman selling the mare for a few months, and once I'm in the arena, she passes off the lunge line with a flirty smile.

I dismiss her attention with a nod, then shed the stress of being around Pops like a disposable layer, but my skin isn't that thick. Most days, I don't even care he's not proud of me. All I want is for him to trust me.

I move to the center of the arena and let the mare have about thirty feet of lead. My frustration comes out in how I hold the line, and the mare's neck lifts as her back hollows.

Releasing a slow breath, I focus on the mare, who reverts to perfect form. I turn my shoulders forward, away from her, and step into the movement I want her to make. She picks up the cue. A man can learn as much from a horse as a good horse typically learns from a man, and for a moment, we are totally in tune. I anticipate her movements before her hooves drop. It's like our hearts are beating to the same metronome.

"Let Davis do it," Pops yells.

"Why?" I yell back, making the mare stall her gait.

"I don't like how you're leading her."

"But I'm good at this."

"Not with this mare, you're not. It's total resistance, and she looks miserable."

*She does now.* I shout, "Fine." What else will I say to the all-powerful Charles Corbett?

I may hate Davis for taking the farm foreman job that used to be mine, but I hand the horse over to him and tell myself it's fine. Fine. Fucking fine.

Anger wafts off me as I pass paddocks and chicken barns. A tractor rumbles past, its grumbling engine as loud as my thoughts.

Nudging my anger toward acceptance, I walk toward the house. The outer walls are hand-plastered and smooth in the afternoon sun. Rock cut from the property paves the steps leading onto the veranda.

It's a massive old house and another storied part of our family's tradition and history. Inside, I head for the kitchen, get a glass of water, then continue past the sitting room and west veranda. Intent on getting to my room and taking a cold shower, I strip off my T-shirt and rub it down my stomach to absorb the sweat.

Voices echo against the walls as I approach the great room. Preferring not to step in the middle of one of Nonna's visits with her homesteaders' little kids or hear about being shirtless, I stall outside the threshold to get a read on the conversation.

"He's adorable," Nonna coos. When I peek inside, she's leaning over a little boy, making kissy faces.

I hate my grandparents' homesteaders. Not just because it seems like Nonna is trying to replace her family with all these newcomers, but because Dad hated Pops's agenda, giving our land away to outsiders, undermining our family and traditions. It's what Pops and Dad were arguing about the night my parents died.

The festering wounds are torn open by Nonna's interest in their offspring. One day, if Pops gets sick and passes before her, she's going to give everything to the children of these homesteaders, as if blood and heritage make no difference. She sees them as her future. I would argue with them if it got me anywhere. Instead of tormenting myself, I head back outside, taking the roundabout way to my room, which has an exterior door.

My dogs must sense I'm back and available to give them attention, because they leap around a tall hedge and greet me with excited yelps. Job whines for a rub down, and I oblige him until he rolls over and lets his tongue loll out. Kim, an Akita like Job, sits on one ass cheek, waiting for her turn to be loved.

"If only my life were so easy," I mutter, "I could be happy."

I rub her down, too, contented by their easy affection. When I was in jail, I missed these dogs more than any of the people in my life.

Even as most of my life goals feel hopeless, I must be determined, careful, and patient. I want to be the heir. I may have zero privacy and self-worth close to the film left in a trough after a cow's tongue has licked the tin, but my suffering is worth the sacrifice, because one day, West Creek will belong to me.

If I'm smart enough to win them over. And winning Nonna's attention may be easier than proving myself to Pops.

To get Nonna's attention, I need a wife.

I may need a wife, but I want Christa, who won't go to dinner with me.

Still contemplating the strangeness of my relationship choices, I head for the shower.

Letting my head fall, water drips over me and into my eyes. I swear I don't cry, but my eyes get hot, and it's hard not to feel broken when I let my forehead rest against the colorful Spanish tiles. I stay that way for a while, heartbroken by all I've lost, wondering when things will return to how they were. If they ever will.

"God." I gaze at the ceiling. "I could use a break right about now. If you'd be kind enough to spare me a moment."

I'm toweling off and trying to reinforce my resolve to keep going step by step. Keep it basic. Keep my temper. Stay focused.

My phone rings with a local number. I grab it before it goes to voicemail. "Hello."

"Hey, it's Christa."

*Holy shit. I'll pray more often.* "Hi, darlin'. Glad you came to your senses."

"Actually . . . I'm calling to ask for a favor."

"A favor, huh? Okay, let's do it."

She hesitates as if realizing I didn't ask what the favor is, but then she pushes forward and says, "Well, the thing is, I was hoping you'd say yes. I don't have a lot of time to talk. I'm at the hospital with my dad and met the cutest little boy who wants to be a cowboy. He asked if I knew you, and I said yes." She tells me about Jake's wish to be a cowboy for a day and his leukemia. Once she's done, she says, "Can we get together and talk about it?"

"How about tomorrow? You can come to the ranch?"

"Um . . . Okay." I can picture a pretty flush on her cheeks. "I have to work until four. Can I come after that?"

"Sure, I just want one thing in return, but we can discuss that more tomorrow."

"I'll tell him you'll help me," she says, amazingly sweet and thoughtful.

"Good." As we hang up, I'm smiling so big. It is good. It's fucking great. She can't walk away from me now. Not until she sees this through.

I'm not sure how I got so lucky. I guess God was listening to me in the shower, which seems crazy even to me, but I'm not about to second-guess it.

# CHAPTER 7

CHRISTA

DAD'S RECORD-KEEPING system is as disorganized as the burn barrel we keep for trash.

Abandoning a half-complete insurance audit and ignoring the past-due notice about our EPA permit, which could shut us down, I jump in my truck and head for West Creek Ranch to meet Carter.

The sun glares in my face despite the visor, and I'm so late that I feel terrible about it, but when I texted him earlier, he said it was no rush. *Get here when you can.*

He still hasn't told me what he wants in exchange for helping me make Jake's wish come true.

My fingers tap restlessly against the steering wheel. I'm edgy about asking Carter for help. I'm curious about him even though I shouldn't be, and I smile when I think of him even though I try not to.

He's a nice guy. That's why he agreed to do this.

I glance nervously at the visor mirror. No makeup. No hair-spray. Mom would be disappointed in me. Skyler was adamant that I needed to stop by her salon so she could make me up, but I don't have time, and what's the point? Maybe this way, Carter will see what I look like most days and lose interest.

The thought makes me sad. Since Carter came back into my life, I'm a mess of conflicting desires ranging between an intense need to focus on the tannery and a strong desire to see where this could go.

It's maddening.

On either side of the road, West Creek Ranch is intimidating, with green pastures and fences for miles. I approach the main gates, broad arches formed from adobe plaster the color of sun-dried earth. Split rails hang between matching posts lining the long gravel driveway.

Carter said to meet him near the arena, so I continue past the huge low-slung house toward a row of whitewashed bunkhouses, then past long buildings that must be chicken barns, then paddocks lined with weathered boards. Finally, after dodging a few cowboys who cast curious gazes in my direction, I park near an arena with a timber announcer box and a matching grandstand.

I talked to Emily last night and got more ideas about what Jake might want, then put together an outline for Jake's wish. I printed two copies and brought them along to keep our meeting efficient and professional.

Grabbing the papers, I hop out and shut the door of my old truck with a soft clunk.

Carter must have been waiting for me because he comes down from the top of the bleachers. His muscular shoulders are familiar, while something about his swagger is impossible to replicate outside their family. Their granddad walks precisely the same way. So does Max.

But those thoughts are just a distraction; Carter's coming

toward me, and it's like being stalked. He could be here to help or devastate, and the uncertainty is almost unbearable.

With the sun setting, the wind is starting to kick up. He continues toward me at a slow walk, and I grab my flyaway hair and put it into a low ponytail.

As soon as he's in earshot, I ask, "What's your one condition?"

He approaches until he's standing close. His eyes are crinkled in amusement. "You're pushy, aren't you?"

I put my hands on my hips and cock my head to one side. "I like to know what I'm dealing with upfront."

"Have dinner with me tonight. My grandparents will be there." His steady gaze unhinges me.

"Sure." I'm not dressed for dinner! Will that matter? Carter's not dressed up. I'm unsure what to do with myself and unwilling to make another move for fear it will be the wrong one. I stare at the plans for Jake's day. None of this would be possible without Carter's help. I glance up and find him fixated on the ground between his boots.

The wind stops, and it's quiet. Areas like this, near wilderness, are never truly silent. Breezes rustle. Birds soar against the colossal sky. Beneath the leaves, insects work their magic.

Carter moves his boot against the ground, and I study him while he's not watching. He's dressed almost the same as he was at the rodeo. Dark jeans. A short-sleeve button-down shirt with a collar and pearl buttons. A belt with a buckle big enough to serve dinner. And he looks oddly vulnerable, as if he cares how I answer.

His vulnerability makes me say, "Thank you for asking me out the other day. I'm sorry I couldn't take you up on it."

He smiles at me in a way that makes me want to see him smile like that again. Soon.

"What's this dinner going to be like? Do we have to convince them to let us have Jake's day here?"

"That part won't be hard." He frowns.

"What are you worried about?"

"You've met my grandparents?"

"Yeah. Of course."

"What's not to be worried about? They're generous to people like Jake but hard on Max and me."

"That seems backward, doesn't it?"

Carter shakes his head and smirks. I've amused him, and he likes it. "Backwards may be Pops's forward. Trust me. You'll understand by the time dinner is over."

"Might be fun. I've wondered why they do the homesteads."

"How about you don't bring up their homestead program?"

"Sure."

"Please don't upset them," Carter says.

"I'll do my best." *What have I gotten myself into?*

If a look could convey all the words of a grateful heart, the one he sends me tries. "How's your dad?" he asks.

"Stubborn as ever." I smile, even as the memory of how Dad was after his appointment makes me want to cry—not pretty tears either, but those big wet, red-faced tears.

"Yeah."

"He doesn't let me go to his appointments, so I don't know what's happening except what I can see." And what I saw . . . I blink the image away.

"You're worried about him."

"A little." I offer what I hope passes for a reassuring smile.

He must see how close I am to tears, and it makes me want to cry even more, and I hate that weakness in myself.

"You've been home a couple of months?" he asks, giving me an out.

"A few. I'm really happy to be home. Everything is going to get better real soon. I'm sure of it."

"Christa." He says my name and waits for me to look at him. "Stop trying to act like everything's okay when it's not."

"We should focus on Jake. This . . ." I lift my hands and motion to myself, "it's not important."

"You are important, and you're upset."

His phone chimes. He doesn't move to see what someone wants. Instead, he's staring at me, attempting to show me he cares with a look.

Staying silent doesn't feel right, so I talk. Too much. "My dad has always been strong. He refuses to let anyone help him. He still insists on driving his truck instead of spending money on a van equipped for his wheelchair. He can barely walk." Remembering how Dad slid down the side of the truck as he tried to maneuver into the seat makes tears threaten again.

"Well . . ." Carter takes a breath. "He's lucky to have you back home."

Hearing Carter echo what everyone else keeps saying is crazy-making—not just because I have a hard time accepting praise but also because it's not true.

I can't stand having him look at me like he is now, so I launch into the truth, admitting the disaster I was in New York. "I lost my rowing scholarship. Then I spent an extra two years finishing my degree because I had to work full time."

"Oh." Carter's voice is quiet.

That alone is enough shame, so I don't tell him that I eventually got arrested for punching my sexual harassing boss in the face, then threatening to gut him, or that the condition of my deferred sentence was leaving town.

"I can't lose focus," I say, reinforcing my argument. "There's too much at stake with my dad, sure. But it's also my student loans, and the tannery needs a major turnaround. I'm not sure how long we'll be able to keep it open if I can't figure out how to ramp up production and bring in more orders." I have to fix the tannery for him, and maybe I'll just stay there and run it forever. *With no reference, good luck finding another job. Maybe I am stuck here.*

Carter presses his lips together as if he's trying not to respond with his instinctual answer. His phone chimes again, but he doesn't move. I don't think he's even breathing.

"I shouldn't have said all that." I'm proving myself to be a nutcase. "Please don't tell anyone."

"You can trust me." He says it so earnestly I believe him. He will keep my secret.

My awkwardness and self-loathing melt. He's not judging me like I thought he was.

Something hot and ugly builds inside me. I'm not sure what it is. Fear? Relief? I push my thumbs into my eyes. A little gasp escapes on my next breath. I'm not crying, but I want to. I need to.

He steps close. I put my hand on his shoulder to hold him back, but he puts his warm palm over it, holding me and keeping me balanced. "I can understand why you won't go out with me."

"I owe you an apology."

"You don't owe me a thing."

I look up at him for a split second. I'm about to cry again. Before I do, I suck in a breath and look past him at the arena. So picturesque against the mountains, I'm sure it's been in magazines. I'm friendly and grateful to everyone under normal circumstances, but Carter is different. I've dreamed of kissing him since elementary school. I look at his lips and feel the same strong pull, dormant inside me all these years.

"I understand what it's like to have a mission and not want to let anything get in the way." He scrubs a hand over his face, then shakes his head as if recognizing my resistance and pushing his desire away. "What do you say we work on Jake's day for a while and come back to this?"

When I agree, he starts toward the arena, saving me from myself.

I walk beside him, trying not to feel too much while laying out some ideas from my plan, including roping lessons, a pony ride, a cowboy outfit, and a cookout.

"What do you think?" I ask.

"I like it. What if we start with practice in the morning to show him around, then turn it into a festival like they do with those medieval fairs, bring in everybody on the ranch, maybe a few folks from the rodeo?"

"That sounds incredible."

He pauses to smooth out a rut in the gravel road with his boot. "Which parts do you have figured out?"

"The costume, mostly, unless you have any ideas, and a pony unless you have one."

"Sounds good on the costume. I'll see what we have too, and no offense, but I think the boy would prefer a horse."

"He's a little frail."

"We've got several gentle horses. What if we let him meet them and choose? They can bond a little. I always enjoyed that part when I was a kid. Still do, I guess."

"Okay. I trust you there. What do you want me to do?"

"Maybe we should put an exam together, so he has to earn his cowboy status?"

"I could do that." *I think.*

My stomach grumbles in protest of my not eating since before lunch.

He smirks. "I take it you're ready for dinner."

"I could eat."

We walk toward the house in companionable silence. It's much more comfortable being around Carter now that we've talked for a while.

"How'd you like college?" he asks.

"Ithaca's ranked the #1 college town in the US, so . . . it was fun."

"You miss it?" He casts a sidelong glance but looks away before his gaze locks with mine.

I answer truthfully. "Not as much as I thought I would." I don't tell him that being home is getting easier because of him. Maybe I wasn't cut out for my old life, but I miss having independence and believing I would do something meaningful with my time.

"What'd you like best?"

"The lakes. You probably could have guessed that, and I do miss rowing."

"You still want to leave a mark on the world?" He grins.

"You remember that?"

"You're the one thing I tried not to forget from that summer."

Heat builds in my chest, making it warm and tight, reminding me how much I liked him and how hard it was for him after his parents died. He planned to rodeo full time, but after they were gone, he lost a lot of his spark. I hated seeing him like that, but a memory of him smiling at Mandy Morgan makes it hard for me to believe him now.

"You wore a fur bikini." He blesses me with a wicked smile.

"I still have it."

"Bet it looks even better now."

Even though I wonder what he's up to, I can't help how I'm blushing or smiling. He's changed from the guy I remember—still nice but a lot more aggressive and confident, more bravado than the painfully polite guy I knew in school. "You're smooth, aren't you?"

"You ought to see me when I hit my stride."

"Humble too."

"My humbleness is my favorite thing about myself."

"That right, your humbleness? Has a nice ring to it."

He looks down like I've embarrassed him. So, his confidence has limits too. Hoping to keep our conversation going, I change the subject. "Still want to join the circuit?"

"Nah. I wouldn't have liked it anyway."

"What do you want to do now?"

"Get married to a pretty girl who's smarter than me, settle down, run the ranch, maybe have a few kids. How's that sound?"

"Um. Good. That's . . . I expected you'd be married by now. Doing all those things you just listed."

"Been waitin' on you, darlin'."

*Have mercy.*

"Dating doesn't have to be a distraction." His brows are drawn like he's contemplating a puzzle.

For me, dating has always been a huge distraction, so instead of addressing his statement, I ask, "Why me?"

"Because you're special. The way you talk to me is different. Like earlier, when you asked me about my rodeo dreams, I bet you weren't thinking that I'm too old to go out on tour now or that I've been in jail and have probably thrown away my chance of ever amounting to anything. I bet you weren't thinking about how little of my potential I've realized or that my kids will grow up knowing their dad did time. That's why."

His eyes are tight. There's a seriousness there and a sadness I can't quite understand.

I reach out and barely catch myself before I touch his arm. Still, my body leans toward him. Even my feet point at him like Carter Corbett is my true north.

"When we were in school, everyone else talked about my parents, how miserable I must be since they were dead. You talked to me about what I wanted. Even if you want to deny it, I bet you remember that as well as I do."

"I remember." It feels like I'm admitting so much more. "I really liked you back then, but I still can't date you, though. I am sorry. I just can't. Even being here costs me the time I should spend at the tannery or with my parents." Or leaving town.

"Two people focused on the same goals can make a real difference in each other's lives. Think about the classic couples."

"Like who?"

He frowns and rubs his chin. "Bonnie and Clyde?"

"They were bank robbers."

"During the Great Depression." He offers me one of his life-altering smiles. It really should be a crime to be that good-looking. His light-colored gray eyes are like heated silver. Mesmerizing.

Captivated by how his attention is fixed on me, I smile back and consider my stance on bank robbery. I'm not really in favor of it, but I can see what he's trying to say about couples being successful together.

When I don't say anything, Carter says, "Guess I've thought differently about things since I went to jail. Rules don't mean as much to people when they're desperate to do the right thing, especially when it comes to helping the people they love. Their family."

"Is that what Bonnie and Clyde were about?" When I say it, I feel like I'm accepting that part of him, even as I wonder how the nice guy I remember ended up there.

"Yeah." That one word seems to state much more.

He is magnetic.

I have to put my hands in my pockets to avoid touching his sexy forearm.

Maybe he sees how hard it is for me to resist him because he's persistent. "How about Johnny Cash and June Carter? They were married for years. What would have happened if she wasn't there to change his life?"

"The world would miss that movie about them. Plus, they had some great songs."

"Right, like ''Cause I Love You.'" Carter lowers his voice. "You should listen to that song."

"Okay." Heat pools inside me. It's like he's given me a gift, not just any gift, but the right one. I left home swearing I was not too fond of country music, but I listened to an A.M. station at night when I got lonesome.

"We're gonna make that song come true," he says.

My throat is so tight that I barely say, "I guess I'll listen to it, so I know what's coming."

"You better do that." He leans toward me and runs a finger down my cheek.

# CHAPTER 8

## CARTER

Christa's dark lashes flutter, then she presses her lips together and averts her eyes, scanning the fields behind me. I try to mimic her by staring at the side of the house. We're only a few feet from the kitchen door—that close to being inside, and I've already looked at her long enough to memorize everything.

Silver pearls rest around her neck with a turquoise pendant shaped like an upside-down horseshoe. Her hair is in a messy ponytail, and there are holes in her jeans. I guess that her panties are pink, just like her lips. I move toward her just an inch.

She presses her hand to my chest to hold me off but doesn't push me back. The warmth of her hand so close to my pounding heart feels right. Still, I'm not sure what to do. Give her space or claim her mouth.

Her lips are parted. My breath comes faster. I lean in until my mouth is a fraction closer. She moves toward me, closing the gap until we're nearly touching—my breath quivers. I swallow the urge to move. Her exhale teases my lips.

I close my eyes, and she's still pushing me away when her mouth meets mine. I open to her immediately. She tastes like summer, heaven, and every good thing I've ever known. She's in my arms, and it's a fantasy come true. I crush her to me. She runs her hand up my chest to my neck, pulling me into her.

My tongue finds hers, and I'm lost in the wetness and hunger of her kiss. Because I'm done living halfway, I pull her hips to mine, showing her what she does to me.

She breaks away, flushed and breathing hard. "We shouldn't be doing this," she says, pulling me into her again.

I deepen the kiss with everything I feel about us. How right we are together. How she can make me whole again. How much I need her to try.

"Carter, where've you been?" Pops asks in his typical commanding tone.

Christa and I spring apart like adolescents. Before she's too far away, I grab her hand and bring it up, placing a kiss on the back.

None too pleased with my failure to answer him, Pops repeats himself. Repetition is never a good omen. Yet, at the moment, part of me is hard-pressed to care. If he criticizes me in front of Christa, it will end my temper-keeping streak.

Christa's smile might melt even Pops' glacial heart.

*This girl is all I'll ever need.* The angel on my shoulder tries to remind me that I'm getting ahead of myself. She kissed me, sure, but she doesn't want to date me, much less marry me. The thought steals the life out of my breath, enough that I'm disoriented and trying to catch up with the conversation when Pops leads us into the house.

As we stand in the kitchen, Pops is as frosty as Wyoming in winter. Still, because he likes to talk about himself and the family name, he gives Christa the tour, explaining that the house is named the Castilleja Mansion, after the Indian paintbrush, a flower that grows wild in the spring. Whitewashed adobe walls are smooth, and natural light floods every room. The floor plan resembles an old fort with a formal courtyard. Every room has a view of the ranch or mountains, and most have exits to a wide veranda that frames the courtyard.

Pops talks non-stop. "It's been the Corbett family residence since they built it in 1896. Our forefathers cut stone from the property to make accents on the mantel." He points at a massive fireplace with a domed mouth and a slanted stone chimney. "Nearly all the furnishings, custom wall paneling, and built-in features are original. At the time of construction, it had a central heating system, nineteen fireplaces, hot and cold running indoor water, indoor flush toilets, and a refrigerator room in the kitchen. All of which were novelties at the time."

"I've seen nothing like it." Christa runs her hand down the sloping arch of one of the doors. Soft, rounded tops fall inward to corbels that act as supports from the ground. On the thick inner walls, between rooms, there are candle pockets.

She gives me a long look, then shakes her head and stares at the tile floor. I'm not sure what it means. Maybe she's impressed or maybe she's wondering why she let me talk her into this. Either reaction seems equally justifiable. It is a great house, but Pops is a lot to take in.

He's oblivious and still talking as if he doesn't realize the tour might make her uncomfortable.

Finally, he finishes his monologue and leads us into the main dining room. Nonna sits alone at the far end of a table that can seat sixteen. The newspaper perched in front of her face makes it look like she's been waiting for a while, rearranging commas in *The Talisman,* a newspaper they publish that hardly anyone reads.

Sometimes, I think she has the patience of a saint to put up with Pops and the rest of us. Maybe me, especially.

Nonna looks up with green eyes that turn from weary to

sparkling a second before she crumbles a page into a ball and tosses it at Pops.

"Just a few more articles." Pops bats the paper to the floor. When he looks at her, he grins. Even after fifty years of marriage, they're in love.

Pops rubs the bridge of his nose, and Nonna frowns at him and returns to the copy edits.

They both look so old now. Pops still parts his gray hair down one side, the same way it has always been, but wrinkles crease his neck. Sun has thickened the skin, and time has stooped his posture.

"This is Christa Blackburn," I say to Nonna.

"Yes, Christa." Nonna pauses, as if she needs to reset herself. "It's been too long since we've seen you. How are you, dear?"

"Good, but busy. You know how it goes."

"We do, and how's your mother, Meredith . . . No, Melody, is that right?"

"Yes, that's right. She's . . ." A flush creeps over Christa's cheeks, and her chin dips before she pulls it up and says, "She's been good. My dad's illness has been hard on her, but she's managing."

When they ask about her dad's health, engaging in a series of back-and-forth questions, she tells them it's a type of multiple sclerosis paralysis that affects both legs. Then, when they ask about the tannery, she explains how she's working on getting larger contracts and broadening their operations to generate more revenue so they can qualify for a loan to modernize.

"It must be hard on all of you," Pops says. "We heard you're back to take over the tannery."

"I wouldn't say take over. Not exactly."

"Well, sit down," Pops extends his hand, motioning to the table. "Tell us about it."

Christa gives me an imploring look, begging me to rescue her from an interrogation.

"Let's eat. I'm starving," I say. Everyone thinks I'm an asshole anyway.

"We were waiting for you." Pops's eyebrows do that thing where they turn to point in at the top, like Jack Nicholson's in *The Shining*.

"Your arena is beautiful," Christa says. "The way you positioned it against the mountains is stunning."

Conversation turns to how lovely the weather has been. Then the ranch cook, Kay, comes in with a tray of salads, and talk turns to the flavor of the food and how nice it is when people grow their vegetables.

Nonna's very proud of her heirloom garden and could talk about it for an eon. All I can say is I hope no one mentions the homesteads. I don't want Christa to feel awkward talking about a program she doesn't understand, and if it comes up, I'll do what I can to spare her the lectures I've endured.

Following up on my conversation with her earlier, Nonna asks about Jake. "Do you know how sick he is?"

Christa sets down her fork to answer. "Emily said he's stable, but no one's sure how long it will last. We all have our fingers crossed."

"Oh, poor thing," Nonna coos. "We should do his wish quickly. Maybe this weekend?"

"We need more time," I say. "There's a lot to do."

Christa lowers her chin and lets out a breath. "Emily said with their appointments and her work schedule, it would be best to do it next Wednesday."

I should have asked this earlier. I was thinking we'd have a month to plan and pull it off, but this means I have *seven days* to make the boy's wish come true and convince Christa she likes having me around. When I look at her long and hard, it's like she feels my intensity, because she turns and offers me a little smile. It's one of those bittersweet smiles. Maybe she regrets kissing me.

I'd do it over, though, because it still feels right.

"How does your homestead program work?" Christa asks.

I groan internally. Why? Just why can't anything in my life go smoothly?

She directed the question at Pops, who props his elbows on the table as if settling in for a debate before answering. "What do you mean, specifically?"

"How would a person like me apply?" she asks.

I was not expecting that, and by the looks of Pops's frown, he wasn't either.

"Have you read *The Talisman*?" Nonna asks.

"A little." Christa nods.

Nonna refolds the copy she was editing and slides it across the table. "Take this. At the back, you'll see the ad. That's where people find out about the program. Then, if they're interested, they send applications."

"Thank you."

"Good." Pops nods. Crisis averted.

"To be honest," Christa says, "I've read the paper and found it intriguing, but I've never liked the program because it brings in people who aren't prepared for what it's like to live here."

"She doesn't mean that," I say, unsure how she misunderstood my unspoken request that she impress my grandparents. Maybe I should have spelled it out?

She smiles at me, bright as the sun, melting my agitation. "I actually do."

*Well, shit.* Bringing Christa may ruin my efforts to impress the grandparents, but I like Christa. I care about her. Maybe no woman I like being around will ever please Pops. Maybe it doesn't matter.

"What you're saying," Pops says, "is you're concerned our program will change the local culture."

"I've seen it change our culture."

"And you don't approve."

"It seems like a cult."

I scrub a hand over my beard.

The room goes eerily quiet while Pops's breathing gets loud and his face goes red. "It's a philosophical organization dedicated to virtuous living. Not a cult."

It's so quiet, the air conditioning sounds loud.

Nonna laughs. It starts as a mirthless chuckle but builds into something more cheerful. Within seconds, she's almost giddy.

Pops turns toward her, baring his teeth.

"Oh, Charles, stop being a stick in the mud. You've got to admit she's funny."

Pops stares at Nonna.

"It is a little like a cult." Nonna's mirth grows until they're both overcome, laughing heartily until they're almost crying.

They've finally lost it. I lean back in my chair and shake my head.

"Do you know how long it's been since anyone but me spoke to him like that?" Nonna asks, but it's a hypothetical question. No normal person speaks to Pops like that. *Ever.*

I glance at Christa. Even though she doesn't like their homestead program, they like her for speaking her mind.

"Have you considered how much better people would accept your program if it benefited locals?" Christa asks.

Almost in unison, they look at her.

"Can't say I've given a lot of thought to what people think of me," Pops says.

"But we're not opposed to local people becoming homesteaders," Nonna adds, softening his admission.

"Never have been," Pops confirms.

"What about a homesteader who doesn't fully abide by your principles but shows promise in other areas of life? Maybe they understand the ideas but aren't willing to embrace someone else's philosophy about how they should live."

Nonna says, "Charles is always trying to convince our newcomers to think more independently and question what they're told."

"They need to think for themselves," Pops says, "and find

their authentic belief system or they'll lack intellectual agility and forever struggle to maintain motivation and focus."

"What about your grandsons? Are they free thinkers or true believers?"

I give her a look, *what the hell?*

"Carter lacks self-discipline," Pops says as matter-of-fact as a dictionary.

He stares at me like a stern look will drive the point home.

I send him a matching icy stare. Can he not see how much self-control it takes for me to sit here and act like I don't hate him for not understanding me?

No one lifts a fork or chews.

Every day, I make small concessions to appease him. It shows I have endless self-control. Even now, I'm exercising it as I keep from saying what I'm thinking.

Christa puts her hand on my knee. Maybe she knows I'm barely hanging on to my self-control.

She squeezes in a quick gesture of support then focuses on Pops and Nonna as she says, "You may think Carter lacks discipline, but I see a man who is persevering on inner strength. He's been to jail, been judged by a community and his family, all while remaining committed to what he believes."

Pops releases an indignant sniff. "It's what he believes that's the problem."

"What you're saying is: Carter lacks self-discipline because he doesn't agree with you."

"He refuses to admit when he's wrong."

"Says Pot to Kettle," Christa says with a gleam in her eye. Then adds, "My dad *always* says that to me."

Pops crosses his arms over his chest and stares me down as if I'm responsible for putting her up to this. While part of me wonders what the hell just happened, I sling my arm over the back of her chair. It feels like a victory.

"I hope I haven't offended you," Christa says.

Pops says, "I'm not so obtuse that I can't see the argument you're making."

"Maybe we can work out a deal so their tannery can process West Creek's hides." I draw the heat of Pops's irritation. "We'd have to build a processing plant and stop selling overseas."

His animosity could make a horse bolt, but I shrug it off, almost smiling at how dinner's turned out.

"I suppose we could look into it," Nonna says.

Kay brings in grilled chicken with more salad to keep Pops's cholesterol in line, and the rest of the meal passes with remarks about current events as if the momentary awkwardness hadn't happened.

"Thank you for having me over," Christa says.

"It's been interesting," Pops replies. "Tell your folks we said 'hello.'"

"I will. My dad said to come by if you want to see the taxidermy he's working on. He's got a few ideas for your bear."

After the way she's been able to corral Pops, I'm even more taken with her.

"How'd you do that?" I ask as soon as we're outside. It's dark, and I pull her toward me so we're both in the light from the small lamps along the paved pathway.

"I've read their newspaper."

"No shit. Maybe I should read it too."

"You probably should if you want to figure them out."

I shake my head in amusement. "I thought he was going to have a heart attack when you asked him if the homesteads were a cult."

She smiles.

It feels good to release the tension. "How did you know you could do that?"

"Your grandparents may be loaded and sheltered, but they're genuine, hardworking people. Being questioned makes them think."

"You were serious about helping me." I think back to the

condition I laid out when she got here this evening. What I didn't say aloud but hoped she understood: *Help them see I'm not the fuckup they think I am.*

In the moonlight, with flyaway hair and a gleam in her eyes, she looks more alluring than ever, or maybe it's how whip-smart she is.

"When should we get together again to work on Jake's wish?" she asks.

"Are you going to let me kiss you again?"

She gives me an unreadable look, and I shrug in an attempt to say, *All my cards are on the table darlin'.*

"Are you going to answer my question?"

"Every day until the big day. Now, will you answer my question?"

"It happened so fast."

"I'll be honest, Christa, I've wanted to kiss you for years."

She puts her hands out as if to keep me away. "That's sweet of you to say," then she turns on her heel and heads toward her truck. I've scared her.

I walk beside her and feel so much that I can't find a thing to say that doesn't seem corny or too aggressive. It tests my patience when I shut the truck door behind her.

When she's on her way home, I stare after her taillights.

I want her.

I never cared to impress any woman the way I want to impress her.

Living in the main house, down the hall from my grandparents, is what I thought I wanted because it's my best shot at becoming their heir, but my life isn't very independent. To attract a girl like Christa, I need privacy and a place of my own—soon.

# CHAPTER 9

## CHRISTA

ONCE I'M STOPPED behind the tannery, I search my phone and bring up a video of Johnny and June singing "'Cause I Love You." I shouldn't listen to it because Carter never said a word about being into me years ago. He's proposing now after hours together. I've lived long enough to know a line, but I'm curious. Besides, old twangy country is not my style, and I need to see what a fool I am, falling for Carter's lines like it's the first time he's ever said them.

*That's my excuse, anyway.*

I press play, and it is an old song, not my typical taste, but the lyrics are so direct and intensely personal that I stop the video halfway through, because watching Johnny and June sing to each other gives me all the *feels*. The lyrics about loving each other no matter what, listening to each other, and supporting each other through all of life's beauty and pain—I huff out a breath of pent-up desire mixed with painful longing. I jump out of the truck and head inside the tannery. *Focus, Christa.*

I spent a whole day with him, which I should have spent working—nothing like processing a stack of deer hides to get my priorities straight.

The first half hour is torture. Sitting behind a sanding machine, shaving thicker parts out of one hide after another, does little to occupy my mind.

Instead of feeling like I'm accomplishing something, I feel stuck—dissatisfied with my life, thinking about what it would be like if the Corbetts offered local people opportunities instead of recruiting outsiders.

At dinner, I had meant the questioning to help Carter. Perhaps with prodding, his grandparents would see him as worthy of their attention, but now I'm thinking about myself again. Getting on our feet financially might give me room to have a relationship without feeling like my every emotion will be the catalyst that leads Dad into bankruptcy. If I can just focus, I'll sort this out and get back to New York.

I need to stop wanting things I can't have and concentrate on my responsibilities. Being around the Corbetts brings out all my worst qualities. Lust. Greed. Envy.

I wanted to impress Carter, maybe a little too much, and during dinner with his grandparents, I lied about our business success—*We're making progress. Have a few big contracts in the works.* Why lie, except that I'm so unhappy?

My gaze trails over the open-topped tanks we use to prepare the hides, then to the stacks of boxes containing orders from customers who've preserved their furs with salt to prevent them from rotting until we get them into the liming vats. This isn't a glamorous gig. The process consists mainly of adding a series of chemicals to soften hides into finished furs.

Carter offered to build a processing plant to help us, but why?

Does he pity me? Or does he care about me the way he says he does?

Carter wants a wife. He said as much, but I want security that can't be found relying on a man.

But maybe I could rely on Carter. Even if it's scary, I could try. What if I did?

I close my eyes, imagining what that might look like, and momentarily lose focus on the sanding machine. That fast, the wheel burns a hole right through the hide.

Shit! Shit! Shit! Not only did I cut my hand open, but I ruined some hunter's trophy, and I'm so screwed.

I'm at the first aid kit, trying to stop the bleeding, when my phone starts ringing.

"Hey, Mom," I answer, holding the phone between my ear and shoulder.

"Where are my car keys?" The hard edge of her voice sends a twinge of fear right through my eardrum.

"You're not allowed to drive, remember?" She's not forgetful, just manipulative. "The doctor said you can't drive while on Xanax."

"I stopped taking it."

"But you need it, for—"

"I hate being out of breath."

"Have you had any vodka?" Shortness of breath is one of the side effects of combining Xanax with alcohol. Last time I saw her, she was mixing a screwdriver in a thirty-two-ounce tumbler.

"Only two."

"But you didn't take your prescription?"

"I don't remember."

I stop wrapping my hand to focus more fully on what Mom's saying. "Do you think you're having a reaction?"

"Maybe."

"You know it's not okay to drink while you take your medicine, right?" The whole point of the medicine is to help with withdrawals from drinking.

"Don't lecture me, Christa. I'm a wreck right now."

"Why tonight? Why now? Wait . . . Where's Dad?"

"He's lying on the floor."

"He's what?" I finally snap.

"He won't talk to me."

"He won't talk to you or can't talk to you?"

"I don't know. He's not talking!"

"Why didn't you tell me?"

"I did. Why do you think I need my car keys?"

"Hold on." I'm frantic now, rushing toward my truck and prepping to dial 9-1-1, knowing we're over an hour to the hospital by ambulance and we can't afford a helicopter ride. "I'll be right there."

I send Skyler a quick text, then squeal to a stop in front of my parents' house, throw the truck in park, and leap out, putting all things out of my mind except Dad.

"Where are you guys?" I yell as soon as I'm over the threshold.

"What's all this?" Dad asks, lying behind the kitchen table.

"Are you okay?" I sink to the faded linoleum floor.

"Of course, I'm fine." He squeezes my wrist reassuringly.

I study him for a long moment, and he does look fine, no worse than when I saw him earlier in the day, except that he's on the floor. "Why are you on the floor?" I ask.

"I asked your mother to let me have a moment of quiet."

"So . . . Can you start at the beginning?"

"No!" Mom yells at me from the doorway into the living room. "We do not need our daughter in the middle of our argument."

"Melody, shut up." Dad lifts his head to yell. "Christa should know."

"Know what?" I look between them. It's then I notice the suitcase in Mom's hand, the way she's dressed to the nines, with lipstick so red she looks more made-up than I did during the rodeo after I let Skyler work on me for two hours.

"Why are you holding a suitcase?" My voice sounds shaky, like it did when I was nine and they split up for the first time.

"Goddammit, Leland," Mom mutters. "Why couldn't you just give me the fucking car keys?"

I glance at Dad. He closes his eyes.

I stare at the peeling daisy wallpaper until it blurs.

Mom digs through my purse until she finds my keys, then holds them out. "I can take your truck, or your father can give me the keys to my Mustang."

I stand and stalk toward Mom, shaking my head in disbelief. "One of you better tell me what the hell is going on."

"He's filing for divorce," Mom says. "It's his punishment for my drinking. I finally get to escape this hellhole once and for all."

It might be for the best if she leaves, but I'm more concerned about what life might be like for her without Dad.

"Where are you going?"

"Your father doesn't care." Mom shrugs. I recognize it as my own. It says, *I may hurt, but I don't trust you enough to show it.*

"Come on, Mom, why not sleep on it?"

"No."

"If you still want to go tomorrow, I'll drive you."

"I want my car. It's in my name. I'm allowed to drive it."

"Not when you're under the influence."

"There's no alcohol in the house!" she yells.

"I poured it all out," Dad says. "But it was too late."

"Fine, I'll go buy a car!" Mom yells.

I want to yell, but instead of anger, sadness spreads over me the way dense fog envelops low-lying valleys. The kitchen door rattles, and I wait for someone to walk in on a classic embarrassing family moment, but no, it's just the cooler kicking on, making the house groan from changing pressure.

Keys jingle in Mom's hand. I can't let her take my truck. Not when she's been drinking.

I grab my keys before she can react. "You're not taking my

truck. It's in my name. If you wrap it around a tree, I barely have insurance."

"You're just like your father, talking about insurance. Money is all that matters." Mom pushes past me and storms out the door carrying her suitcase.

I should have offered to let her stay with me and Skyler, but our trailer is so small. I don't want Mom to stay with us. Skyler will want to know if I offered. But Skyler is a terrible influence on Mom. They shouldn't even be around each other when Mom's like this.

Dad finally struggles to push himself up. Once he's sitting, he asks, "You okay?"

My chest is tight against my inhale. "I'm fine."

Dad pulls the chair next to me and struggles to get into it.

Dammit. I want to yell at Mom for being so nasty to Dad when he's sick, but I also want to yell at Dad for not leaving her a decade ago. I want both of them to leave me alone so I can go back to the tannery and forget about their drama.

He squeezes my shoulder and repeats, "You okay?"

I hate that my life feels so totally out of control, that I've made such terrible decisions, that my parents' lives are such a mess, and that I'm back home like I'm still nine years old and unable to do anything but mediate. "Are you getting divorced?"

He offers a half-clenched smile, then exhales long and slow. "Probably not."

I shake my head, disgust and anger building a hornet's nest in my stomach. "Maybe you should."

"It's not her fault," Dad says. "It's how we were raised."

*And this is how you raised me!* I want to yell, but I don't, because it wouldn't do any good, and Dad is sick.

# CHAPTER 10

## CARTER

IT'S WAY LATE, and I'm standing on Christa's parents' front porch with her mother, who is drunk. The porch lights aren't on, so it's dark except for stray window light, the moon above, and an occasional car.

It's not a big house, but with flower pots on the steps, it's well-kept compared to the neighboring homes, which are a little run down, with peeling paint and overgrown yards.

Christa's inside, or so her mom says as she squeezes my bicep.

"I like your tattoo." She runs her finger over it.

"Mrs. Blackburn, where'd you say Christa is?" I ask again, hoping she'll get the message that I'm here for her daughter and let me inside.

"WC." She traces the letters as she says them. "Is it your family's brand?"

"Yeah." I brush her hand away, but she seems too drunk or too determined to get the point, because she puts it right back where it was.

"Christa's a great girl," I say, trying to get her motherly instincts to kick in.

"She has a lot of student loans."

"I'm sure she'll pay them off. She's really smart." I step toward the door. I should knock.

"Christa's alright," Mrs. Blackburn blocks my step. "She takes things too seriously. I'm always trying to tell her. Have more fun. Stop being afraid of every little thing."

"I want to help Christa have fun. Maybe take her out sometime."

"Why don't you take me out? I'm a lot more exciting."

I tell myself to breathe. There has to be a way out of this that doesn't include running for my life or hurting the feelings of the woman I want to marry by being rude to her mother.

Fighting every battle is a luxury I can't afford.

So, I establish priorities. First, get Mrs. Blackburn to unhand me. Second, support Christa. Third, find out why she texted me with an SOS. Twenty-third, figure out how to forget this strange encounter with her mother ever happened.

That's when Mrs. Blackburn says, "I've always thought you Corbett men were handsome."

I grunt.

"I bet you have a belt with your last name on it too." Mrs. Blackburn leans on my shoulder. Her breath is near my collar. "Maybe I could see it up close."

Mother fuck. I push her back as I step away.

She's not having it, though, and clings to me as she kisses my neck and whispers, "No one will hear us if we have sex out here."

I hold her by the upper arms and try for logical. "Well, I'm here to see your daughter, and you're married."

"I've already had to have a little fun on the side."

The adrenaline rush from earlier recedes. For as much as I can drink, it's strange how much I hate the smell of booze. Even though it's not real strong, it grates on me. I start to feel physically ill at her proximity and the situation unfolding, mainly because of what all this means for Christa. Is she dealing with this every day? Her whole life?

Deciding I'm no longer obligated to Mrs. Blackburn's feelings, I release her and step forward, intending to knock. "I'm not interested in you. Not tonight. Not tomorrow. Not ever."

"Why not?" She steps so close there's no path to the door without touching her. "I'm attractive, right?"

Christa lives in a truly nightmarish household. How can I help her with her mom like she helped me with Pops?

Is there a way? I'm not as smart as Christa, but to hell with all of it if I'm not determined.

I open my mouth to talk some sense into Mrs. Blackburn, but she pulls her dress down and her lacy black bra is on display.

What should I do?

Unwilling to turn around, I step back. Escape may be my only option to avoid making this a whole lot worse.

Christa comes to the door, and I know what it looks like. She yells, "What the hell?" Running outside, she sees me—who I am—and freezes.

It's a perfect storm, and I have no idea what to do about any of it.

I'm momentarily too stunned to react.

Mrs. Blackburn yells at Christa. "I want my car keys. I want them right now."

She's the same sort of person as the guy who killed my parents—unhinged by alcohol and about to get in a car.

"Talk to Dad about it," Christa yells back. "He has them."

Mrs. Blackburn stomps past me without another word and heads into the house. This is the opposite side of alcoholism impacting a family, and witnessing it is strange, almost surreal. Christa is the barrier. Maybe I should leave? Let them sort this out? I've been up since before dawn and have to be up early again in the morning. By the time this is over, I won't sleep.

But I want to help. I don't want to let the night end like this. I've never been one to run from a fight.

Christa puts her hands on her hips and glares at me. "What are you doing here?"

My defenses perk up. A wolf cornered, but I try to sound calm, collected, and in control. "I came to make sure you were okay. I got a text."

She flinches back. "From my mom?"

"No!" My tone hits that peaked defensive note I was trying to avoid. "From you."

"I don't understand. What did it say?"

I pull out my phone and show her the text.

> Christa: Dad's unresponsive. I'm headed to their
> house now. DPY

She reads it, then deflates. "I meant to send it to my cousin, Skyler."

"Well, shit." I was in the barn playing my guitar when Christa's text came through. I had been strumming Johnny Cash songs and trying to sing—not that I'm any good, but the process relaxes me. I saw those words, and it seemed like she understood I would always be there for her. Whatever it takes.

"It doesn't say come over."

"No, but I thought you might need help."

"DPY means 'don't panic yet.'"

"Oh."

She lets out an exasperated breath. "I'm sorry about my mom."

I'd been worried she would ask and I'd be forced to explain, but it seems she knows. Without permission, my hand moves up to rub my neck and comes away marked by Mrs. Blackburn's lipstick. "It's no big deal," I say, even though I've never thought of drinking and driving as *no big deal.* "I think she's a little drunk," I add, because *yeah,* but also because I want Christa to talk to me.

She covers her face, and her hand is bandaged but still bleeding.

"How'd you hurt yourself?"

She pinches the bridge of her nose, close to tears, with wet eyes and trembling shoulders.

I want to wrap her in my arms and tell her that her pain is my pain. I connected with her all those years ago, and I want to do that more now, but if she won't let me do that . . . A new worry builds. I may have misread Christa from the beginning.

I hold out my hands, palms up, not quite surrendering, but close.

If we could just talk, maybe we could find common ground. I offer again, acting on the instinct to help. "I can fix that up with the kit in my truck."

"I don't . . . I can't . . . I tried to tell you I didn't have time for a relationship. I tried to be nice and polite, but you can't seem to understand, and now I'm going to be blatant and maybe a little rude, given how my mom can be, but frankly, I don't have the energy for *this.* See how much of a disaster my life is? If tonight doesn't make it clear enough, I don't know what else to say."

"I get it, and I'm sorry for interrupting. I'm sorry for how things looked with your mom. I'm sorry I don't have a better way of explaining what happened."

"You don't have to apologize." She shakes her head. "I'm the one who accidentally sent you a text. Now I'm yelling at you. I owe you an apology."

I shake that off. "You don't owe me a thing. It's been a long night, and I don't blame you for being upset. You've got to be tired too. You worked all day, spent hours thinking about Jake, had dinner with us, then went to the tannery and worked for who knows how long, and now you're here helping your parents. I get it, you're running on fumes."

I try to show her with a look how well I understand her and how important it is to me that we talk through this.

"Did you listen to that song?" I ask. "Because I'm here for you."

I follow her gaze to the neighbor's camper, where a dryer sits outside.

She releases a heavy sigh. "I did listen. I liked it."

# CHAPTER 11

## CHRISTA

*I'M HERE FOR YOU.* Carter's words bounce in my brain like a foreign language I'm trying to decipher using my phone's translation app, except I'm unsure of the mother tongue.

I admitted to listening to "'Cause I love you," and now, Carter knows I liked it. If it's just a line, he should bottle it as an aphrodisiac and put it on the market.

He fixes me with intense scrutiny, making me want to crawl into a hole and die, but instead, I smile.

"Can I help you with your hand?" he asks.

"Sure," I agree. I'm not in a shambles over having him stay in my parents' front yard to examine my embarrassing life. Nope. Not me.

The tilt of his eyebrows and slight uptick of his mouth are burned into my mind even after he turns his attention to retrieving something from his toolbox. With him facing away, I admire his broad shoulders, the cotton sleeves hugging his biceps, his tucked-in shirt narrow at his waist, and his still-perfect ass. Whatever this is between us will end as soon as Jake's wish is granted, but I can enjoy the moment and keep my guard intact.

But he will move on eventually, and it will hurt. An anxious buzz of nerves awakens in my stomach. Any path I choose will be wrong. The knot in my throat threatens to choke me, while my heart thumps wildly. This may not be life or death, but it's a different kind of danger.

He switches on an enormous light that brightens the bed of his truck, making me feel like I'm under a spotlight while he fishes around in the toolbox.

I order myself to stop freaking out and watch him instead. I'm lucky he's here. I will remember this night forever. After how he reacted to Mom, without peeling out of the driveway or laughing, I might need to reevaluate my beliefs about men.

He retrieves a scuffed canvas bag with orange straps, then comes around to the back of the truck and lowers the tailgate.

"Mind sitting up there?"

I shimmy onto one side while he opens the bag, exposing a well-used first aid kit stuffed with professional-looking supplies.

"Let me see your hand." He holds his right palm out, a big hand with long fingers and callouses from working his rope.

He's going to see my frostbitten pinky, which I hate. Even though he might remember from school, I hesitate before laying my injured hand in his, curling my fingers to hide the scars from view.

If he notices, he doesn't mention my awkwardness. He pulls me toward him at the same time he steps closer, his thigh settling against my knee, making it impossible to think of anything other than the feel of him touching my hand and leg. One side of my body is totally alive.

He pauses to look at me as if studying a wild horse for clues. With his attention and touch comes a wave of desire that makes me intensely aware and anxious about what he will do next. "How'd you cut yourself?"

"I was distracted at the tannery."

"I can't imagine why." One corner of his mouth ticks up, and I know he's thinking about my mom, but I don't want him to believe I only think about her.

"I was thinking about you." Anyone would hear the longing in my voice. I shouldn't have said it, because I'm sending mixed messages like a nutcase, but I don't regret it because he almost smiles.

"Does it hurt?" He starts to peel away the bandage.

"Not much," I lie as the adhesive gives way, making me tense.

His grip is warm and gentle, and I try to relax. We're both wearing jeans. His are newer, and mine are so faded they've developed tiny holes at the wear points along the seams. He's doing the nice guy thing, looking after me because I'm hurt, but it feels like more. No one ever notices when I'm hurting, much less takes care of me.

He lowers my arm, brushing his fingers against my upper thigh, and a low hum builds behind my belly button, branching out until it seems he must be able to feel the vibration. I hold my breath. I'm ultra-sensitive, recalling his fingers against my neck when we kissed, wrapping in my hair and pulling me in. I lean toward him just an inch.

He notices because he offers a slow smile. "Want to tell me what you were thinking about?"

*Not a chance.* "Are you a traveling doctor?" I ask, deflecting.

He tilts his head then smirks. "I volunteer with the fire department."

"You're a firefighter?" I ask.

He nods.

"You are a nice guy." I regret saying it, because it implies I thought he wasn't.

"You're a nice girl," he says with enough heat to power my fantasies for a month.

When our gazes lock, I feel extra alert, like he's about to say something important, and he does. "It's part of my court-ordered community service. After my folks died, I thought being a firefighter would make me feel better. If I was out there helping people when they crash or whatever."

"Does it?"

"Sometimes."

Not wanting to ask him about his jail time but curious, I say, "I remember hearing you got in a fight. Was it with the guy who killed your parents?" That's what I remember hearing.

After a pause, he says, "I did what needed doing to keep him from killing someone else."

"He was still drinking?" I ask, ashamed of Mom for trying to get her keys while under the influence.

"Stumbling in the parking lot at Bertie's and about to get in his car."

"I'm sorry you got into trouble for that. It's crazy they put you in jail."

"Try telling that to my granddad."

"He thinks you got what you deserved?"

"According to him, I should still be in jail. The other guy did time in jail and is now also in a wheelchair, so I shouldn't be walking around. It's . . ." He purses his lips.

"I think I understand. Not that I agree with your granddad, but I can see how hard it would be for you to accept his point of view since the same guy killed your parents, and he's still alive. Just because you put the guy in a wheelchair doesn't mean you should be in one too."

His eyelids droop, making him look a little despondent. Instead of agreeing or debating, he says, "I should focus on your hand."

I want to say, *Sorry about what happened to you, and sorry about my mom. We try to keep her from driving when she's like that,* but I don't want to think about her or talk about her right now. I glance back at the porch.

Silence stretches between us, but it's comfortable. With the bandage off, the gash is bleeding again, deeper than I realized.

"You might need stitches," he says.

"I don't think so." No way can I afford an emergency room visit over a flesh wound.

"What'd you cut it on?"

"I burned it on a sanding wheel. Fleshing a hide."

"I've had rope burns like this," he says. "I'm going to clean it, then put a ZipStitch on it."

I must look confused because he hands me a packet of sutures and says, "I'll pull the paper off, then center it over your cut, stick it down, and pull the sutures until they're closed."

I can't help the awe in my voice. "You're a traveling doctor."

"Not quite." He grins.

With careful, deliberate movements, he cleanses the cut with a spray, then allows it to dry before applying the sutures, breaking off the small tabs used to tighten them, and placing a sterile bandage around the side of my hand. With no needles, it doesn't even hurt.

"Thank you," I say quietly once he's done. Then starting to babble, I add, "You should probably get going. I bet you have an early morning."

"It's the least I could do." He's gone completely above and beyond what any average person would have done, and I'm not quite sure how to read him.

"Why is it the least you could do?"

He rearranges the supplies in the gear bag, setting aside several bandages and a few extra sutures. "I'm going to give you some things so you can keep an eye on it. An ointment will help, but if it starts to get infected, you'll need an antibiotic."

"You're not going to answer me?" I ask, flirting.

His eyes dance with amusement. "I'd bet you were thinking about kissing me again."

"That is *so not the case*." I smile an I've-had-a-crush-on-you-forever smile and blush.

He sighs audibly, all flirtation. "It was a great kiss."

"Come on." I slap his arm with my good hand.

"Admit it." He reaches out and grabs my wrist, then looks at me through hooded eyes with long lashes, asking whether his touch is okay. I lean toward him at the same time he shifts forward.

"I won't admit it." I cross my legs below the tailgate and draw them in.

His gaze shifts to my mouth and he groans hoarsely, then steps between my legs, which open on their own, his hips pressing against the inside of my knees. "When you texted me about your dad, I was thinking about you. Figured you must have listened to that song and understood that I would be wherever you need me."

Heat spreads from the pressure of his knees up my thighs and between my legs. All he's done is bandage my hand and tell me he wants to be wherever I need him. My abdominal muscles pull up and in at the thought. But there's a voice in my head reminding me of how easy it is to fall and how bad it hurts. He's not going to stick around once he knows how bad things are all the time.

"It's a good song." My voice is harder than I'd intended. "But how many girls have you reeled in using that line?"

Carter stiffens, his brow losing its playful quirk. I can't tell if he's offended at being called out or hurt. Either way, I expect this is the end of our good time. Some of the buzz drains from my limbs as my body relaxes into the idea of going home and climbing in bed alone, but the relief is suspended, because instead of getting defensive or pushing me away, he runs two fingers up my wrist, then up to the tender spot inside my arm, stopping at the crook of my elbow.

Trailing his fingers back down my wrist, he asks, "You really want to know?"

I can't find words, unsure of what I want because having him answer might mean he stops what he's doing, and it feels *that* good. Waiting for an answer, he lingers in my palm, where his touch would tickle if the pressure wasn't perfect. Instead, it makes me crave his next move as he shifts, focusing on each of my fingers with adoration. My body responds like it's the first time anyone has ever touched my skin. Desire. Curiosity. Craving.

Even if he's used his lines a million times, I'm not sure I want to know.

He lifts my hand and places my palm flat on his chest, pressing in with his palm on top so I can feel his heartbeat is fast, like mine. "You wonder what kind of man I turned out to be. I know I did a lot of stupid stuff when I was younger, but I've grown up. Maybe faster than I was meant to, and I probably changed more than I realize. Being locked up in the county jail over in Wesley, I had a lot of time to think about what a stupid fuck I'd been."

"You weren't stupid." It's the quirk of his eyebrows that makes me add, "You were that nice guy all the girls wrote about in their notebooks when they were practicing their new last name."

He smirks, but just as fast his expression resettles into seriousness. "I didn't know much. The point is, you're the only one I've ever told about that song, and you're the one I thought about when I was spending time with other girls back then, but I wouldn't have admitted it."

His reasons from back then are exactly why we won't work now. We are from opposite ends of the social spectrum in a small town where stuff like that still matters. I really should stop letting him do stuff like this. It's not fair to either of us when my life is such a disaster.

"I hate you!" Mom screams, bursting onto the porch, the screen door smacking its frame in her wake. "Go fuck yourself, Leland," she says, then storms off the porch.

I pinch the bridge of my nose and shake my head, unsure if I want to laugh or cry.

If I were betting, I'd say she found more booze inside to keep her occupied, but now Dad's found out and he's pouring it down the drain. *Let the games resume.*

"Have a good night," I say to Carter as I resist the desire to cover my face with my hands, embarrassed that he's witnessed exactly how low he'd have to bend over to stoop to my level. When he doesn't move, I add, "You should go."

I'm confused about how I got here. Not the day itself; I know that part. I mean to this point where I'm so focused on Carter. What will working with him on Jake's wish day be like? That's where I'm headed, so I'll find out.

It's hot and stuffy in the truck, so much that it's almost suffocating. I don't have air conditioning and want to roll the windows down, but I'm on the phone with Skyler, and we won't be able to hear if I do. I just finished explaining everything that happened last night because she was over at some guy's house and wasn't home when I got in.

"He bandaged your hand. Then you told him to leave?" Skyler asks.

"I said, 'Have a good night.'"

"'Have a good night' like *with me*," she lowers her voice into a sexy purr, "or 'have a good night' like I don't care if I see you again?"

I inhale long and slow, maybe because I want to conjure an answer that will satisfy her, or perhaps because I hate how I left things with Carter. I finally shrug off the weight of regret and say, "The second one."

"What did he do?"

"He said, 'Alright, I'll see you tomorrow.' I don't think he wanted to leave."

"Oh . . . That's good. You still have a chance."

"I don't want a chance. I want to give Jake a good wish day and move on." But even as I say the words, I know they're not true. I hate having Skyler pick apart my feelings. "I can't stand having Carter know what a mess my life is. I want to crawl in a hole and die."

"I know," Skyler says. "But you can't. Clearly, you understand the opportunity in front of you."

"To date Carter, because that's all you can think about."

"He's hot and rich." She's just like her mom, living the high life, too fixated on stuff like this. Still, Skyler's always had a life worse than mine, with no dad and a mom too self-absorbed to care what her daughter does.

Deflecting, I say, "He's sweet and genuine." And that's the real problem. He's too good to be true, like one of those beauty infomercials Mom watched last night after I finally got her to calm down.

"I just need more time with Max," Skyler says, changing the subject. "He's a little cool, but I'm sure I can warm him up."

"God, I feel sick. I'm rolling down the window." If only the cool air coming into the cab and cleansing my lungs could fix everything going wrong with my body, mind, and life. My stomach buzzes with nerves.

"Fix things with Carter," Skyler says, "whatever it takes, and see if he'll tell you what Max thinks of me."

"Okay," I say, because it's the only way I'll get her off the phone. "I've gotta go. I'm parking now."

Carter is waiting for me at the arena, leaning against the rail like he owns the place.

No sense in prolonging the inevitable. I shut off the truck and step out.

I'm so embarrassed that he saw what my life is like that I can't look at him. Instead, I focus on the ground, my hands, and the paper I printed about Jake's day.

"How's your hand?" he asks.

"Better." I look up and meet his mesmerizing eyes. The concern in them washes over me like a salve. I want to thank him specifically for making my night better, but vague seems safer, so I hold up the papers like a shield. "Thanks for your help last night. Let's work on Jake's day. Okay?"

Carter doesn't miss a beat and makes planning easy. I imagined store-bought decorations, a cowboy outfit, and a pony ride, probably using a rope since I'm not an expert with horses, but Carter's got a whole plan. He's intelligent, intuitive, and focused on making Jake's day more amazing than I could have imagined, coming up with ideas like a trail ride, "losing" a few head of cattle to create a round-up and finding an impromptu shelter to spend the evening outside. Then cowboys would show up and tell stories around a campfire.

"It's pretty awesome." I rub my hands together.

"Would he want to invite other kids his age?" Carter taps his pen on the bench between us.

"I'll ask Emily." I write it down on my list of things to do. "How can I help with all this other stuff?"

"We'll need supplies for the shelter. Somebody's got to figure out the food. The rest of it's pretty easy. It'll only take me a few hours."

"I can handle the food and shelter." It can't be that hard.

"Want to start right now?" He offers me a hand as he stands. "We can stage the campsite."

I accept his hand, feeling it would be wrong not to, and am instantly greeted by a flicker of electricity. His eyes widen slightly. Either he's registered my reaction, or he's having one too. Maybe both.

Either way, he lets me go. We walk toward his truck in silence that carries as he starts it up and takes off past the busiest parts of the ranch to rolling fields where cattle graze.

The inside of someone's car can offer a glimpse into who they are. Carter's truck is new enough to smell like a car lot. I've never had a new car in my life. I could count the number of times I've been in a new car on one hand.

Carter's life seems like another world from where Skyler and I live.

"Tell me about Max," I say.

"He's my little brother."

"I never had a sibling. Is it that bad?"

"He's fine," is all the reply I get.

If I go home with nothing for Skyler, she'll never let it go. She can be as determined as Mom's terrier on a treat, only less adorable.

"Skyler is sort of like a sister to me," I say as a segue. "She gives gifts no one wants."

He turns to me and smirks. "Like what?"

"One time, she gave my dad an electric eyebrow razor."

He laughs. "Nothing says happy birthday like shave off that unibrow!"

"Awful, right?"

"That is pretty bad. So, what else has she come up with?"

"What else? Last year for Christmas, she gave my mom a stripper pole."

"Holy fuck." Carter snorts.

"As if she needs any encouragement, right?" It feels okay to laugh about it with Carter, even if making fun of my family makes me hate myself a little. I guess it's pretty raw.

He grins. "What'd Skyler give you?"

I mime zip my lips and barely contain a smile because no . . . Carter does not need to know about the sex toy my cousin bought me for Christmas.

"Damn, it's good to see you smile again," he says.

"It's nice to see you smile, too."

And we're smiling at each other like lovesick fools.

He stops the truck in a low-lying area near a creek. "What do you think of this spot?"

It's pretty, with a thick carpet of blueish-gray grass and big trees offering plenty of shade. But specializing in nuisance wildlife, I focus on the plugged culvert and muddy slide right in front of us and say, "Looks like you've got a beaver or two living here."

"Yeah." He lifts his brows. "Probably so."

"We could move them," I offer, because that more humane approach has been my contribution to our trapping business. Beavers aren't as annoying when they're not destroying things people care about.

"You don't sell the pelts?"

"We do, but it's not my catnip. The tannery is my dad's passion. I'm not especially fond of hunting, trapping, or even tanning. I'll do it, but I don't enjoy it like some people."

"You don't have fur curtains around your bed?"

I snort. "Are you disappointed?"

"A little." He stares at me with a tilted head and an undecipherable expression. I hold eye contact, wondering what he's thinking. It's not about taxidermy. Is he imagining us together in bed? If he is, I should stop staring back at him.

But I'm still staring, lost in what it felt like to kiss him. It feels like we were just kissing, but also like it was an eon ago. Was it only yesterday?

He has so much allure that I can't resist him for more than an hour without feeling overpowered by a desire to touch him. What will I be like a week from now? A month from now, I'd be lost entirely.

Squeezing my sore hand, I remind myself how much a distraction could cost me. Once the ache is intense, I say, "We better get to work."

And we do, for an hour. They've got a dugout-style cabin tucked against the sloping hill. It needs a good cleaning but is otherwise perfect enough to be out of a Western movie. While I fix up the inside, dusting and sweeping, Carter focuses on resurrecting an old fire pit.

At some point while I'm inside, he takes his shirt off

because when I come to the door to let him know I'm finished inside, he's facing me shirtless. He's hotter than he was in high school.

Not that looks are all that matter, but *have mercy*. He didn't have to be so good-looking. Resisting him would be easier if he wasn't.

I turn around in the doorway to avoid looking at him.

"Christa." His steps crunch against dry leaves as he walks toward me.

I turn back, hoping to avoid embarrassing myself, and say, "I like your tattoo," but my throat is tight, and my voice sounds sultry. Trying to make a joke, I add, "I bet you have a belt with your name on it too."

Carter steps back, shaking his head and turning away from me.

"What's wrong?"

"It's not important." But his face is pinched like he's trying not to laugh.

"It is because you're important," I reply, using his words from yesterday against him. "And something I did is funny to you."

"Your mom said that to me, too, about my belt."

"Oh my God, no! She didn't. Did she?" I don't know if I should laugh or cry. "I was joking . . . God." I hide my face in my hands and want to crawl into that hole I thought of earlier and die.

"It's fine." He pulls his shirt back on. "I know you were joking . . . And I've seen worse drunks."

Of course he has. "I've been trying to help her," I say. "We all have."

"I was trying to help too."

As much as we've talked today, neither of us has spoken about last night. I swallow before speaking because I'm unsure I can trust my voice. "My parents want to get divorced."

"Why don't they?"

"I don't know. I've tried to figure it out. Sometimes they threaten to, but they never do."

"Some marriages will always be like that," Carter replies, and looking at him, talking to him, it's easy to wonder if I could make a life with Carter. Would he be a good, kind, supportive, and loving husband? I don't want to lose a chance at happiness because I'm too afraid, or to spend the rest of my life caring for the tannery, caring about Mom's choices more than she does. What if Dad dies? Is this what he's been trying to tell me?

"I want to thank you for last night." I'm working up my nerve to ask him to dinner, but my pulse thrums in my ears. At the last moment, I hard shift. I don't want to lead him on, and as great as Carter is, as much as it would be amazing to have him in my life, I don't have time for a relationship.

I smile tightly. "I'd like it if we stayed friends. I'm not saying it will be like this forever," I add, like a total nitwit. "I'm just saying I can't be more than friends right now, and I don't expect you to wait for me to straighten out my life. So, we should be—"

"Friends," he says. "I get it. You don't have to explain anymore. I'll respect what you're saying."

It's bittersweet when he concedes, because as much as I thought he would walk away from us, behind his stoic expression, I see his quiet resolve like he won't abandon me for turning him down. Like he sees and understands things I'm only starting to learn.

He bumps my shoulder. "Want to meet my dogs?"

"Sure." I guess that's something a friend would do.

We walk toward the house and are quickly greeted by two large Akitas with thick black and gray fur, burly shoulders, and curled tails.

"They're not always good with meeting new people," he says, stopping them before they reach me, then slowly showing them I'm not a threat.

He didn't have to worry, though. They're sweethearts, tumbling on the grass, playing fetch, and showing silly affection to Carter. Being with them brings out a lighthearted side of him. He plops down on the grass beside me. Job licks me, starting on my hand and quickly moving up my arm to my neck as I laugh and roll toward Carter. He tucks me into his side, pulling me in with his arm before he leans back so we're lying flat on the grass, vulnerable to constant licking.

"This is fun," I giggle, wishing I hadn't asked him to be just my friend but also glad for the pressure it takes off. Now we have ground rules that don't include kissing.

"Have you ever talked to Max about Skyler?" I finally ask.

Carter rolls toward me, studying my expression as if he's deciphering one of those wooden puzzle gifts with money locked inside.

Finally, he says, "A little."

"What does he think of her?"

# CHAPTER 12

## CARTER

WHEN CHRISTA ASKED what Max thinks of Skyler, it seemed like an important question that held the fate of our future relationship in balance.

I lied.

I shouldn't have, but I did.

The conversation is still on my mind two hours later.

I think Max will do whatever I ask, but I need to know.

I don't call ahead before going to find him. That would be typical of me, forcing him to come to the ranch, and the conversation we're about to have will require finesse.

In all brutal honesty, my little brother is fucked up. Has been since the night he knocked the shit out of Cody Harris, the drunk driver who killed our parents.

But I didn't tell Christa that when she asked about him. I didn't tell her anything about the strange bond my brother and I share or how it's made us connected and disconnected simultaneously.

I figure he'll be at Sterling's, his not-yet-open restaurant, which is actually a rundown building. He's been restoring it, but he's not making much progress. Last time I was here, a few months ago, there was an immaculate commercial kitchen but no dining room or customers.

As I push through the back door into the kitchen, not much has changed.

It's still perfect and clean but nearly empty.

Seeing no sign of Max, I head toward the Lynyrd Skynyrd playing in the front of the building and find him on a tall scaffold, reaching up to work on old tin ceiling panels.

"What are you doing?" I ask.

Max jumps, dropping a finish nailer.

"Fuck," he yells as it crashes to the scaffold. "You scared me." A moment later he adds, "Hang on a sec and I'll come down."

We head for the kitchen.

He takes off his tool belt and says, "I figured out that if I freeze these old tiles then bend them, all the paint comes off and the bare metal looks awesome."

The metallic color and raised details are pretty cool, even if it looks like it will take him years to finish the job.

"Want help?" I ask, because when I want something, I go all out to get it.

"Nah, it's late. I was gonna stop soon anyway. Give me a minute to clean up and we can do whatever you want."

As I wait for him, I thumb through his copy of the local newspaper. Because he's tied into the Chamber, he's always up to date on downtown happenings. Me, not so much. After skimming an article about the upcoming craft fair, I switch to the section on current ag trends before settling on the ads in the back and noting Leland has listed the tannery for sale. Not sure what it means, I tuck the information away for future analysis.

When Max returns to the kitchen, he's dressed in fresh

clothes, no different from the Levis and T-shirt he had on earlier, except cleaner, and his dark hair is wet.

"You have a shower here?" I ask.

"Yeah."

"Must be nice. You could sleep here if you wanted."

"I do sleep here."

"Never noticed," I reply, but it irks me that he's got a space of his own while I'm still hanging on at the grandparents' house. Still, I'm on a mission and not easily dissuaded.

I announce the first half of my plan. "I want you to run a chuckwagon at the ranch next Wednesday."

"I'm catering a wedding near Jackson."

"On Wednesday?"

"On Saturday, but I need to prep ahead."

"You need four days to cook for a wedding?"

"This is a big deal," he replies, rubbing the back of his neck, annoyed. "Wednesday is my only day to gather supplies and double-check my plan. If I don't have that time, I might miss something."

"Start sooner."

"I don't get the deposit until Tuesday. I can't buy everything I need until I have it."

"Okay," I say, because I'm picking my battles. Plus, I know Max. He loves kids and won't want to be left out of Jake's wish day.

"What's the chuckwagon for?"

"You're busy remember?"

"Don't do that," Max says.

Is it wrong that seeing him flustered makes me happy? Probably, but I don't care. "Christa met a boy at the hospital, and we're giving him a wish day."

"Like the gun shop is doing for the Jensen boy?"

I shrug because I have no idea what he's talking about. As a felon, I can't even own a gun. Not that the law stops me when I'm out on the pastures of our ranch, but still, it's the principle that rankles. My little brother, who beat a man almost to death, could walk around packing if he wanted to while I have to sneak around about it.

"They're sending him to a Bronco game," Max adds because I haven't responded.

"Haven't been in a gun shop since I got out," I say.

"Oh, yeah . . . Sorry. I didn't mean to say it like that. I haven't been to their shop either. I know from Chamber meetings. Anyway, tell me about this deal with Christa. Are you two . . . ?" He raises his eyebrows.

I smile and offer a glimpse of the excitement I feel about Christa.

"Holy shit, really?"

When I nod, he smacks me on the back. "That's awesome. Tell me what you need for this kid's day."

And here it is, my chance.

"The truth is, we've been working together on this deal for Jake, but she's a little wary of letting me take her out."

"Oh."

"Remember when we went to the lake?"

"In high school?"

"Yeah. I want to take her back to Stiltson Lake. We could take your jet skis."

"Go anytime," Max says. "You know the code to get in there."

"I want you to make us a picnic. Make it special for her."

"Okay," Max agrees. "When?"

"And I need you there to keep Skyler happy. Maybe you could write her one of those poems you write, and—"

"Fuck." Max rubs his neck like he does when he's stressed. "I don't want Skyler to know about Stiltson Lake, or any woman."

"It's one day." *Suck it up.*

"I think you know how fucked up this is, and you get off on torturing me."

He is so self-centered. So entitled. So fucking annoying.

Infuriated, I spring off the counter and step up on him.

He moves back until he's pressed against the counter.

I lean in until I'm right in his face. "You think I'm torturing you? You have no fucking idea what I went through for you. I'm finally trying to get back some inkling of what I had before I went to jail, and you can only see how that's interfering with your plans. Try sleeping in a place where they never shut off the lights or losing your freedom, fuckhead. See how that cramps your style. I can't even touch a gun without violating my probation."

Something behind Max's eyes seems to flicker and die. "Right," he says. "That's true, and I'll do whatever I can to make it right."

"You'll go to the lake?"

"Yep."

I glance around the pristine kitchen. He could put on a real show for Christa. "How about you make us all dinner here sometime?"

"Sure," he says. From the way he's refusing to meet my gaze, I imagine he would marry Skyler if I asked him to.

***

I don't dislike my little brother. Not really. He's brilliant when he's not annoying the hell out of me.

On days like this, when he's doing so much to help me, I regret losing the relationship we used to have. We had this invincible loyalty, knowing we could count on each other without feeling like the scales had to be balanced. It didn't matter if it was the middle of the night and the subject was stupid, we could talk.

Soon, things between us will be right again. Or so I tell myself as I sit on the veranda outside the main house. It's barely light out on Jake's wish day. Even in July, the air is crisp and fresh.

I'm exhausted but also gratified, like today is *my* wish day too.

When I have Christa as my wife and a son or daughter to keep Nonna's attention focused on us, I won't need to prove myself to Pops anymore.

Still, does Christa's friends-only policy know no end? It's been seven days since I kissed her and almost as long since I held her hand.

Will none of this work out the way I've planned? Just like nothing went right that night?

For the millionth time in the past few years, my mind wanders to how things between Max and me got this way. I never considered not helping Max with Cody when he called, making it sound like Cody was dead. It was the only option and would have been fine if I hadn't gotten caught driving Cody to the hospital. That's when everything went to hell. Max wanted to take the blame, convinced he could get people to treat him fairly. He threatened to go to the sheriff—a friendly guy who had coached Max's junior high football team.

I told him he was an idiot. We would have both ended up in jail. Maybe I should have let him spill his guts. I don't know. Cody was hurt badly, but he's alive. In a wheelchair but not dead like our parents. Part of the time, I wish I had killed Cody.

"Carter," Pops says from behind me.

I nearly jump out of my chair. I quickly realize he has no idea what I've been thinking.

"Yeah?" I turn toward him. It takes a painstaking effort to make my face impassive. My hand trembles, and I grip the chair to make it stop. It's pitiful that Pops still makes me feel this intense need to defend myself.

"What time does this wish-thing start?"

I check the time on my phone. "We've got a few hours."

"All right." Pops grumps away. "I'll tell your grandmother to be ready by eight."

Still feeling exposed, I launch myself out of the chair, jump-starting my day.

I shouldn't even be thinking about that night. I should be happy with everything that's gone into this epic day. I should be excited for Jake. It's going to be kickass, and it will bring me one step closer to fixing everything.

I've thought a lot about this boy I've never met. I've seen a couple of photos of him, frail and surrounded by stuffed animals, wearing a hospital gown.

Will he even be able to do the things we've planned, or will our best-laid plans be a reminder of what he can't have? Like the cruelty of making a horse wear a feedbag after it's empty. The way living at the ranch has been for me since I've been out of jail. The way it's been working with Christa while she keeps her distance.

I hope it's everything Jake wants and more than he knows to wish for.

Even as my life continues to be unsettled, I've found purpose in giving Jake a fantastic day.

West Creek's stables and arena are outfitted with enough Americana-themed decorations to be confused with a sold-out rodeo venue. It's been a week of planning, organizing, spending Pops's money, and working non-stop.

By eight-thirty, Christa still hasn't arrived with Jake and Emily, so I try to call her, but it goes right to voicemail.

I work on the details, fussing with the horses and fixing the barn just so. I'm pouring everything into this like this is my wish day too.

Her truck rolls in slowly. Finally, after all the effort, the reward is about to happen. Still, even as I'm inspired to make it memorable, I can't help but feel a little low. Everything that's given me a new purpose has an expiration date.

I've put all my cards on this day, and afterward, she might just walk away.

# CHAPTER 13

## CHRISTA

Through the rolled-down window, I wave at Carter. It's a small gesture, but seeing him again feels like coming home. Attraction courses between us as we try to be friends only. I think it will only worsen the pain when I tell him we're going to have to cut back on how much time we spend together. After today, I've got to get back to the tannery. I still want to try to see him, but the sheer volume of responsibility I've neglected to be here is both mind-numbing and crazy-making.

"Hey," Carter shouts. I can tell he's gotten his first glimpse of Jake through the rear window.

None of the pictures do Jake justice. With full cheeks, a mischievous smile, and freckles, he's wearing a trucker's hat, which reads, "when shit happens." It has a cartoon cow on the front.

Right off, I liked his spunk. Even more importantly, though, he doesn't look sick. Instead, he seems happy and normal; from what I can see, he's already got all kinds of cowboy potential.

A kid can look so okay and be so sick. The fact makes me feel a little ill.

One glance at Emily is all it takes to see she feels the same way. Her dark hair is pulled back from her face, highlighting haunted eyes that stand out because her cheeks are so gaunt. Her smile is so thin it hurts. It's like she's trying to be happy when she wants to cry.

I'm not sure I could have handled a day with Jake if he seemed as desperate as she does.

I park near the arena, and we all get out.

"When do I get to see my horse?" Jake asks, skipping in place.

Grimacing, Emily reaches out to stop him. "Jakey, I know you're excited, but this is going to be a long day and—"

"Please, can I see my horse?" Jake brings his palms together in front of him and sends smiles all around. "I'll take it real slow. I swear." Something mildly desperate comes through in the boy's voice. It's essential to Jake that we all agree, but I'm not yet sure enough of the dynamic to understand why.

Maybe he's just excited, but it seems like more than that.

"Why don't we go ahead and check out the barn?" Carter asks, and I'm glad to see him take the lead.

As he walks ahead with Jake, Emily says in a low voice, "Jake won't be able to walk very well by the time his excitement wears off. He's still in pain from treatment, but he doesn't like to miss out."

Maybe he's afraid he won't get to do everything if we don't rush through it. Or maybe, sick or not, he's just a kid, impatient and eager to have fun.

The barn is a private showcase with whitewashed walls and arched stalls in long rows. Savoring the morning air and the scent of clean straw, I follow Carter and stop when they pause in front of a gate. A nearby mare watches us approach.

"This is Juliet," Carter tells Jake and extends a hand, demonstrating how to interact with the horse.

Emily comes up beside me, and I ask, "Has he been around horses much?"

She shakes her head. "Never. As much as he loves them, even with the therapy group offered at the hospital, I've been nervous. He's ambitious but fragile."

Jake seems taken with Juliet until he moves over one stall.

"Who's this?" he asks.

"Max's horse, Baby," Carter replies.

"Does she sit down?"

"Yeah."

"Which one is yours?" Jake asks.

"Duke. You want to see him?"

In all honesty, I'd bet Carter has about ten horses of his own. He had at least that many in high school. So why is he leading us to the big horse who trampled my table? I thought we were going to show Jake quiet, gentle horses.

"Duke's a hell of a horse," Carter says, "way more impressive than Baby."

I grab him by the arm and give him a look. "You're not—"

He grins at me. "I've got this."

"You're going to let him ride Duke?" I ask like, *You think that's a good idea?*

"I was going to introduce him to Monty, a bulletproof Appaloosa. He's a few stalls down."

"Oh."

"Relax," he whispers near my ear. I melt a little more when he squeezes my shoulder.

Duke is all male. Big and beautiful and hot-mannered. He snorts when Jake reaches toward him, and the boy laughs but quickly moves past.

We visit all of Carter's horses. Twenty-two that he's working with as part of his father's breeding program, the ones he rides, and those he's retired over the years.

Monty's stall is at the end of a long row, and we find him near the back wall, asleep on his feet. He barely comes forward. Even when Carter enters the stall and tries to motivate him, he's stubborn and slow.

I put my hand on Jake's shoulder and lean down. "Did you like Juliet best?"

"Yeah." He smiles, but once I take my hand away, he rubs the spot. I'm still trying to figure it out when Jake looks at Carter and asks, "Can I ride Baby?"

Carter's lips roll in as he tries to smile, but he shrugs off whatever emotion he's trying to hide. "I'm sure Max wouldn't mind."

He puts a halter on Baby. Then Jake leads her out of the barn. With Jake and Emily ahead of us, I walk beside Carter, noticing his arms crossed over his chest. I reach out and squeeze his bicep then pull him to a stop and whisper in his ear. "Want to hear a joke?"

When he raises his eyes to mine, instead of gray, they seem pale blue like the sky. In them, I see strain, glittering like the sun between the clouds.

He inhales deeply and, on the exhale, says, "I know how it sounds, but I'm startin' to wonder if anybody's going to want me. If you don't. If you're making me wait and leadin' me on. Darlin', I need to know."

His eyes are so intense with emotion that I'm stunned. He's telling me he doesn't believe I want him. I've been telling myself we could have fun doing this for a few days, but I'm hurting him, and he thinks I'm using him.

"I don't want to lead you on, but I have so much I still have to sort out, with my parents, with the tannery, and this has been fun, and I love being with you and spending time helping Jake, but I can't continue dedicating so much time here. I'm so behind at work. I don't know what I'm going to do."

He holds my gaze steady and earnest. "You're going to listen to your heart. It's gonna tell you what to do."

"Okay." It feels like a release, like ahead, there's a future, and I've made a promise.

"About that joke?" he asks. "Is it guaranteed to make me laugh?"

I pause, trying to get my heart out of my throat and my mind back on the joke I was going to tell, then I smile. Talking about more than the joke, I say, "No guarantees, but it might make you smile. Here goes . . . Knock knock."

"Who's there?"

"Woo."

Raising his eyebrows, he offers a questioning gaze. "Woo, who?"

"Don't get so excited, it was just a joke."

"That was bad," he says, smiling.

"Want another one?" I ask. So it goes. We rejoin Emily and Jake, who join in, and continue until we've exhausted our knock-knock joke libraries.

The mood is light and easy by the time Baby is saddled. Jake reaches for the lead slung over a tall hitching post, and he favors his right arm. Maybe he's even a little pale. Not so good.

Emily is on the phone, giving someone directions, so I help him reach the lead. "You okay?" I ask.

"Yeah," he replies too fast.

"You sure?" I hold eye contact until he looks away. "Does your arm hurt?"

Carter comes up beside me and offers a questioning look.

Emily gets off the phone and comes over. After I explain what's going on, she asks, "Jake, does your arm hurt?"

"I want to be a cowboy," Jake says.

"You will." She kneels to look him in the eye. "I promise you won't have to miss out."

"Okay." He draws out the word like he lacks faith and looks at us with sad eyes that seem to know more than a boy his age should.

"Let me see what's going on."

"We can reschedule," I whisper to Carter.

"I don't want to reschedule," Jake says, trying to hold back tears.

"Find happiness in the small things, right, Jakey?" Emily runs a finger down her son's nose.

He nods, clearly wanting to be strong for his mom, because what does a catchphrase like that even mean to a kid like Jake? I'd have to think about it for an hour to figure out what it means.

"Tell me what hurts," she says.

Jake whines, "My port is sore."

She takes his hat off, revealing his fine dark hair. Then he lifts his arms so she can tug his shirt over his head.

A lump near his collarbone looks like the port he's talking about, and the surrounding skin is swollen and bruised.

"It's gonna be okay," she says, but when she touches the spot, Jake starts to cry.

"I don't want to miss out."

"I know. We just have to check with the doctor." She snaps a photo with her phone, sends it to someone, and stands to place a call. "Dr. Delano's office is super. They'll help us."

Jake tugs his shirt back on, then replaces his hat, and sits despondently as if he's convinced this will be the end of his big day.

As much as I want to reassure him, I can't think of a thing to do or say.

And it makes me feel as low as he looks.

# CHAPTER 14

CARTER

JAKE'S wish day might end before it begins. He's leaning against the bottom rail of the arena's fence. Every once in a while, he kicks so his boot skids against the ground.

Like it's all he can do to keep himself from crying.

Christa's eyes are tight, and her smile is forced like she's about to cry.

And maybe I'm about to make a huge mistake, but I sit beside Jake and wait.

When he looks at me, I say, "Baby was sick when she was little."

Jake's eyebrows draw together in the middle.

"She was born too early. We weren't sure if she would make it, but Max fed her with a bottle for a long time, even after she was big enough to eat on her own."

"He did?"

"That's why he named her Baby."

Jake grins. "Because she's a big baby."

"About a thousand pounds."

We talk about Baby for a while longer. What it was like for her when she was sick. How Max trained her to follow him everywhere he went. She would be sad when he was gone and show appreciation when he returned.

Jake's mood has shifted, and I'm glad to have offered him a distraction when he says, "It's like she's a dog."

"Sounds about right," I agree.

Then Emily announces, "I just heard from Dr. Delano. He says to apply ice for fifteen minutes. Then as long as Jake feels good enough, he can continue."

"Hooray!" Christa smiles. "That's great."

"You think I could get Baby to sit for me?" Jake asks.

"We'll talk about it after we do the ice," Emily says.

"Okay," he agrees without a fight. I'm amazed at how determined he is. How resilient and happy he can be in the face of his pain.

Still, I don't have Baby's loyalty like Max does, so I figure this is one more time I've got to ask my little brother for help.

Of course, Max is all for it and drops what he's doing with the food prep to do what he can.

Once Jake's finished ice therapy, he swears he's no longer hurting.

Talking to Max, Jake excitedly brings up Baby's illness, repeating what I told him.

"She's been healthy for a long time," Max says. "But she went through a lot. I bet it'll help her understand you."

"You'll show me how to make her sit?" He gives Max a smile that reaches his eyes.

"I will. We can't show anybody else, though. Otherwise, she'll be sitting around all day."

"I can picture that." Jake cracks up and then leads Baby into the arena with Max.

The rest of us give them space, relaxing in the grandstand and chatting about what's going to come next and how we can ensure the festivities are as easy as possible on Jake.

Still, everyone watches as Max demonstrates. The first time Jake makes her sit back on her haunches, Emily lets out a joyful cry of amazement. "Did you see that? He did it!"

You can see the pride on Jake's face. I don't think there are words to describe it.

Emily smiles at us. "You've given him more enjoyment than he's known in a long time, and it brings so much joy to me. I could never have done this for him."

As much as I want to take credit, at this moment, I genuinely love and appreciate my little brother. He's the one down there in the arena. It wouldn't have gone so well if our positions were switched, and I'd come out while he showed someone my horse. But Max is different; he may have a hot temper, one furious enough to kill a man, but slights don't aggravate his passion. I think his skin is thicker than mine, and I'd do well to learn something from this day.

The rest of the lead-up to Jake's wish goes off as planned. He's dressed in a shirt closely matched to mine, and his trucker's hat has been replaced with a white Stetson. Around his neck, Emily ties a blue bandanna.

Once everyone is gathered, about fifty people, adults and kids mill around the arena, balancing plates from Max's chuck-wagon while enjoying themselves with the horses.

We file into the announcer's box at eleven o'clock. Jake, Emily, Christa, me, and the grandparents, who are supposed to go first, but instead of offering a welcome and quick blessing of the day's events, Nonna speaks into the microphone, lifting her voice to an energetic tone. "We've spoken to a community member whose brashness has stuck with us, and we want to do more than offer land to worthy individuals, so we're starting a program to support local businesses and entrepreneurs. Individuals with ideas outside of ranching will also be considered for cash grants instead of homesteads."

An energetic murmur carries through the crowd. People are speculating about what this new development means. I glance at Christa, but her focus is riveted on Nonna's back.

"Now," Nonna says, "Charles and I will surrender the stage and let Carter and Christa welcome you properly. Let's give Jake a great day!"

Christa steps into Nonna's place and says, "Thank you so much, Mr. and Mrs. Corbett, for allowing us to enjoy your lovely property. And thanks to all of you for being here to celebrate Jake. Let's give him an unforgettable day!" Short and sweet.

"I think they said it all, folks." We stream off the stage.

I squeeze Christa's elbow from behind. "I'm glad to be here with you. Glad you asked me to help."

"Me too," she says. It feels like one more step in the right direction.

She offers me a small smile as we stand together, waiting for everyone else to stream out of the box.

Only Pops and I are left when he stops me from behind with a hand on my shoulder. "I'm proud to see you've realized the value of helping others."

As good as it feels to have him praise me, I feel guilty. Undeserving. "I haven't done all that much."

"No one has ever become poor by giving. I hope you'll remember that."

We have so little in common that it's hard to swallow that we agree on this. It feels strange as I head down the narrow staircase toward Christa.

Maybe Jake has helped me and Pops find some common ground worth building on.

"You ready?" I ask Jake as we walk to the arena.

"You think Baby'll follow me?" He twists his hands, clearly nervous about our upcoming show.

"I think she trusts you or she wouldn't sit for you." I pause before admitting, "She won't do that for me."

"Really?" Jake giggles. "Cool. I love her." And he skips forward until he's about ten paces ahead of me. I imagine this is like fatherhood, being proud from the background. I suppose there were times when Dad felt this way watching Max and me. I imagine if I'm ever lucky enough to have a son, I will feel like this, but even more profoundly.

As Jake pets Baby and practices, I spend a minute with Duke to get my mind right.

Max comes over with Lily, another of his mares.

Once they stop beside me, I nod toward Jake and say, "He's hit it off with Baby. Would you mind . . . I could ask Emily if it's okay for him to visit her once a week or so."

"I'm never here," Max says. "But if you're up to it, I bet Baby would like the company."

"It'd be great for Jake." And for me. That's the truth.

After that, we start the show. The gate opens, and Jake's holding a Wyoming state flag as he leads Baby out. Max and I flank him, and when we reach the center of the grandstands, we slip horizontally using the saddles' lined handholds to grip as we keep one foot in the stirrup and circle the arena in opposite directions, while Duke gallops free, meeting Max and Lady at the front, where Jake waits.

I lean down and grab the flag from him, then pass it to Max as we cross paths on the next circle.

The crowd roars.

Jake grins and holds up his hands, making Baby walk backward in the center of the arena.

It mostly works out as we'd planned, until I step up on the saddle, gripping the metal horn. Max does the same but then takes it one step further swinging by me inverted with his feet in the air. We get a little wild after that, me going into a death drag against the ground. Max trying to outdo me, which is our way.

I'd love to scoop Jake up and let him ride, or teach him a bit of what we do, and as we meet at the center, out of breath, I hope we do have that chance.

Like a true cowboy, Jake lifts his hat and places it over his heart as he cues Baby to sit on her haunches in a perfect portrait of love.

We leave the arena after a bow and on the crowd's applause.

For the rest of the day, Jake leads Baby around, showing her off to his friends, explaining he can't show them how to make her sit or she'll be sitting around all day. Kids take tests to become certified cowboys and get awarded commemorative T-shirts Christa had made.

It's about as great of an outcome as we could have asked for.

As it's winding down, I stop by Max's chuckwagon to tell him how much I appreciate his help.

He's taken one of Pops's old wagons and outfitted it with a drop-down back for serving deep-pit and stuff he's got going in cast iron off the fire.

"I'm gonna get out of here," Max says as soon as his gaze lands on me. "I've got people lined up to finish serving and cleanup."

I think he's expecting me to argue, but I say, "All right. Thanks for everything."

He smiles, and I know one of these days, we're going to be okay again, which matters to me.

That fast, as if my permission is all he's been waiting for, he turns to the two guys working the wagon with him and lets them know he's taking off, then he says to me, "When you head to the campsite, you might want to take a wagon. Jake's getting pretty worn out."

"That's a great idea." In times like this, I love my little brother. He's considerate and genuine. "You're gonna get out of here?"

"I have to."

"The wedding, right?"

"Yeah." His voice is soft like he's surprised I remember.

"What'd you think of the grandparents' speech?" I ask, still trying to figure out how I feel about it.

He chuckles, shaking his head. "Probably everybody here's going to apply."

"You should be the first one."

"Maybe I will." He grins. "Are you gonna do it?"

"I'll think about it," I reply, but I attempt to put it out of my mind. "Anyway, I'm not dyed in the wool like they want."

"Neither am I," Max says. That's true, but our circumstances aren't the same. He's got his own life, and I'm still hanging on to this one.

I feel stuck again but don't want to let myself go there. So instead, I let Max go and focus on Jake for the next few hours, getting a buggy ready so we can ride around the countryside and still wind up at the campsite as planned.

Most of the crowd has taken off before we leave for our impromptu round-up, leaving only two families close to Jake and Emily with West Creek's cowboys. The grandparents are probably already in bed by the time it's getting dark. Nevertheless, about twenty people remain telling stories around the campfire. Jake and Emily, among friends, seem to have a good time. Once we've exhausted the kid-friendly versions, some of us start playing old honky-tonk songs. One guy is excellent on a harmonica, and another plays a mean fiddle.

It's not too long before people start dancing. Being a total tease, Christa gets up from the log beside me, winking at me before she sways her hips. Right in front of me, so sweet and sultry, I lose focus and touch the wrong strings.

I imagine us together, her dancing while I sing—us dancing. I can see the future unfold like a vision. I want to ask her to dance, but I can't exactly walk away in the middle of a song.

Then a day money cowboy taps her on the shoulder. I watch her face and wait for her to look at me, but she doesn't. I fall into a new vision for the future, where she's constantly doing this—torturing me. As the song ends, I set aside the guitar and grab my water bottle. I'm telling myself that Christa isn't toying with me, then I watch the guy swing her around. Will Christa decide her life is simple enough to settle down? Or do we want things that are too different, putting us on divergent paths?

Jake comes over and sits beside me, startling me when he says, "You like Christa, but you don't think she likes you."

"You know, bud, it's a little complicated."

"That's what my mom says when she doesn't want to talk about my dad. But it's never that complicated. Only adults think things are complicated."

"I guess you're right about that."

He wanders off. And . . . it turns out Jake is a great wingman.

It's time I face the fears that have taken up residence in my head but that I've been in denial about since I was arrested. Hell, maybe it started when my parents died. Regardless of when I started living like I couldn't impact the future, I am officially saying goodbye to living in the past—even if it means I have to take big chances. Try, fail, reflect, and move on. That's my new motto.

I start thinking about that song, the one I told Christa was about us.

I'm yearning for something more, not the least of which is a strong desire to continue seeing her, whatever it takes. I've told her how I feel about her. Our attraction is out of control. She doesn't want this guy. She wants me.

I pick up my guitar, and at the end of the next song, I change it up and start to sing "Cause I Love You"—our song.

It's totally out of character because I never sing in public, and the lyrics are romantic and cheesy. And maybe I'm not a great singer. No one would pay me to sing, especially when I get to the part that's supposed to be sung by June.

Folks around here will tease me about this until the end, but I don't care. I watch Christa step away from her dance partner. She stares at me with wide eyes.

It's a public declaration, and I hope it's not too much for her as she turns away.

Then she walks off.

I lose my tune and am struggling to restart when her sweet voice picks up from behind me with the chorus about how we'll always be there for each other. We start laughing when we lose our place and don't finish the song, but the other guys continue to play as we walk out together.

"That was something," she says and laughs.

Once we're away from the crowd, I stop behind the cabin wall and wait for her to face me before saying, "I couldn't stand watching you dance like that."

She won't meet my gaze but says, "I apologize. I should have thought more about how it would make you feel."

"Were you trying to make me jealous?"

Her eyes snap up to mine, first defensive, then tender. "No . . . Maybe . . . Sorry."

I learned a lot about reading people while I was in jail. The most crucial thing in moments like this is hearing what isn't said. Christa doesn't try to defend herself. She doesn't make me out to be the jealous one. She doesn't say anything; instead, her eyes pinch together like she's trying not to cry.

"Can't you see what you do to me?"

She nods. "I'm sorry. It's . . . I was wrong. And . . ."

I can tell she's about to apologize again, and I don't want her to feel wrong about talking to me. So instead, I ask, "What do I have to do to get you to trust me?"

"I don't know. That's the problem."

"You could ask me for anything, and how would I say no?"

"Why, though?"

"Goddammit, Christa, because I care about you. A lot. More than anything in my life right now." To hell with waiting and being patient. I could lose her if I let her push me away. "What I feel for you I didn't plan, and it isn't perfect. I can't guarantee I'm never going to mess up, but you can't learn to trust me if you keep pushing me away."

# CHAPTER 15

## CHRISTA

CARTER'S RIGHT, of course. It's not that I don't know what I'm doing when I push him away, it's that I've never let myself believe he really wants me, but I hurt him by acting like I wasn't interested in more than friendship. I hurt him by flirting with some guy I'm not even into. All he's done is help me, stay with me, and try to prove he wants me. I want to stop being that awkward girl from high school, who's still hurt that he didn't choose to spend more time with me.

And then, I finally do the thing I should have done back then. I almost can't look at him as I say, "You said the other day that you remember that day we spent talking on the lake."

"The fur bikini." His smile's still there, but it hurts, because he didn't seem nearly so into me back then.

Despite the nerves clawing up my throat, I try to keep my voice light. "It's funny you remember that so well, because for me it seemed like you never saw me again after that day we spent in the boat. I thought we were really into each other. I felt a lot about you."

He shifts a step away, arms hanging at his sides and hands still.

Part of me wants to throw up a shield and say, *I don't know what I'm upset about. It was so long ago; it seems stupid to talk about it now.* But it's still bothering me enough that I don't trust him as much as I want to.

Stepping closer, I tug on the cuff of his shirt and wait for him to look at me. "We'd talk but it was different. It was all about when I was leaving or when you were going to make it big in the rodeo. You started dating Mandy."

He's listening but also tense, squared shoulders and jaw.

"I don't think I ever spent time with you alone after that, but before that, I thought you were into me. Like this."

I look into his eyes and blink hard, trying to get the emotion off my face.

He lifts a hand, cupping my cheek. "I *was* into you like this, but you said you were leaving. That's all you ever talked about, getting out of here, how good you were doing, how much you were looking forward to living in New York, rowing. You had big dreams, darlin', and I'm just here, never leaving this ranch."

So much comes from the hurt in his voice, in his eyes, that his truth is in the words. I pushed him away back then the same way I'm pushing him away now.

I remember my seventeen-year-old self, too ashamed to have a guy over at my house with Mom drinking, terrified of what it would mean to date Carter but still wanting to date him, shrugging off my disappointment that he wasn't as into me as I thought he was, pretending it didn't hurt me. I remember Mom's shrug the other night in the kitchen when she said, *Your father doesn't care.* Her shrug I recognize as my own.

Stretching up on my toes, I wrap my arms around Carter's neck and kiss him. Not accidentally this time, but fully knowing what I'm doing. He kisses me back immediately and settles his hands around my waist, steadying me, pulling me, caressing me. I press into him, molding our bodies into one.

I surrender to the moment, his lips and beard and touch and scent, to a craving that distracts me beyond reason. Kissing him like this soothes an ache inside me. Having him kiss me back makes me never want to stop. He's catching me, caging me, and making me long for more.

With every gentle touch, every swipe of his tongue, he's promising me I can have a love so intense it will break me. When I kiss him back, with so much need that he's pressed against the wall behind him, he meets me with the same energy, convincing me he's strong enough to stay with me and willing to put me back together.

I pour all my feelings into the kiss. Apologizing.

Because I realize, *I'm the one who's been making him feel unworthy*.

The suddenness of it hits me so hard that I pull away, breaking our kiss.

His hat is crooked, and his eyes are soft with vulnerability, and I never want to lose him, even if it means I have to change.

I try to say what I'm thinking, but I'm unsure of the words, and say, "Thank you for taking a chance on us. I haven't deserved you, and I'm not sure I ever will, but I want to prove what you said. That song is about us."

"I'm glad." His words are reassuring, but his flat expression says he's worried.

"This . . . What's going on between us has been fast. Too fast. Most of the time, I feel unworthy of what you say. Sometimes I'm not sure if you're for real or just trying to convince me of something so you can get what you want—which, as flattering as it is, and as hard as it is to admit, I'm not sure you would like me as much if you got to know me."

"Give me a chance. Okay? I may act like I've figured it out, but I'm on a limb too."

"So, we take it slow," I say in my most confident voice.

"We won't lose anything by taking our time," he says, closing in on me.

Something unique and new blossoms inside me when his lips press to mine.

It feels like faith—a willingness to believe everything will be all right. We hit a new level of kissing, exploring, necking, and doing everything to show each other how hard it is to go slow.

His phone blares a warning siren.

"It's the fire department," he says, not quite breaking the kiss, even as he explains there's a call about an accident on the highway. He kisses me one final time, slow and lingering, then says goodbye to Jake and Emily, borrows a horse, and rides off like a crusader.

Watching him go, I still can't quite understand how I got so lucky, and I hope I won't ruin it.

"He's so nice," Emily says.

"Yeah. He is nice." Hopefully, he's not going to rescue Mom from a ditch.

Emily rests her hand on my shoulder, startling me from my thoughts. "Should we clean up?"

She's right. We should. We spend the next hour picking up leftover food and trash, ensuring the campfire is out, and saying goodbye to those who have hung around until the end. One of the cowboys drives our wagon back to the arena. Jake is asleep, leaning against a hay bale with his head lolled back. Emily wakes him to get him in the truck, then buckles him in the child safety seat and sits beside me.

She leans her head against the passenger window. We're all exhausted enough to sleep on our feet. Exiting the long drive-way, I wonder how things are going for Carter. He's probably already met up with the other emergency responders at the accident. Hopefully, he'll find someone scared but only mini-mally injured, like I was when Mom was drunk and ran off the road into a snowbank. We were stuck in the middle of nowhere for three days without a phone or food. Still have the frost-bitten finger to prove it. But it's summer, and someone has already called in help. Most of the time, scary things turn out okay.

Maybe Carter and I can have a relationship; everything will be easier as a team. I imagine a life where every day goes like this one, full of so much good that I can't find anything to be unhappy about. I grip the steering wheel tighter and purposefully aggravate the still tender cut on my hand. It's not so bad anymore, but it won't all be easy. Dad's still sick, Mom's still tricky, and Skyler wants to marry Max. I gaze at the full moon, the lines on the road, then down at my nearly empty gas gauge.

Fifteen minutes later, we arrive at their neighborhood, older semi-rundown homes not too far from the tannery, and I wish I'd thought of something more to say instead of being so silent on the way over. I stop in front of their tiny white house.

Emily opens the passenger door but doesn't get out. "It was an amazing day. Thanks again for making it happen."

"I'm glad it all worked out. Truly, though, Carter did most of it."

She gives me the same mom look I've seen aimed at Jake. "Don't sell yourself short. You two make a great team."

"Yeah, I guess we do." Even as I say it, Carter's mention of Bonnie and Clyde makes me smile. We could be outlaws and stop caring about everything standing in our way.

"He's going to let Jake visit Baby."

"Wow, that's great." A seed of love for this man who sere-naded me and made Jake's wish come true grows into an apple-sized knot in my throat.

"Are you two . . . ?" When I don't respond, she adds, "I don't mean to pry. It's just that anyone could see he's interested in you. And that song . . . I was swooning."

"Me too." Heat moves from my cheeks to my ears, and I'm thankful for the burned-out dome light. For the first time in my life, I feel lucky in love. I'm used to feeling like I have to earn every bit of affection, every hint that I might be valuable, but with Carter, I'm wanted.

"You two are so adorable together." She places a palm over her heart.

It's the first time I've considered what it might be like to have people know Carter and I are an item, and instead of diving into all the doubts inside me, I say, "We're taking things slow."

Emily squeezes my forearm, and her voice becomes animated with passion. "I've seen a lot of cowboys. Hell, Jake's dad's on a circuit career. The only time we see him is when he's on TV."

"That's . . ." I don't even know what to say about a man that selfish.

"Truth is that some men only care about what they want. But not all of them. Look at how Carter put everything on hold to make this happen for Jake. Not because he knows Jake, but because you asked him to. A man like that is special."

"He is special." Part of me would do anything to be with Carter. Runaway, even if it meant we were together.

"But you were dancing with that guy."

"I was." I wait for Emily's judgment, feeling I deserve whatever she says.

"I don't pretend to know what made you do it. Love is complicated. All I'm saying is Carter's a catch."

*Don't let him get away.* She doesn't say it, but I read the rest of her thoughts from how she studies me, like she can tell I've got issues.

"I can see that." This is getting repetitive. "I'll try not to do anything stupid."

"Oh, I'm not saying that. Not at all. I didn't know if he'd done something. Or . . . Anyway, it's none of my business. I'm getting carried away talking about it like I have any idea what you two have going on. I'm no relationship expert."

Emily pushes the door the rest of the way open, gets out of the truck, and goes to the rear door to retrieve Jake.

I glance back at the still-sleeping boy. "He's a doll."

"Jakey." She leans over him and grabs his hat and boots from the seat. "We're home."

"I'm tired." He finally wakes, groggy and groaning as he half-slides, half-falls out of the truck and drags himself toward the house.

"You're right," I say to Emily in a quiet voice. "I've been terrified to take a chance with Carter. It's . . . He seems too good to be true, but I can see what my life will be like if I push him away. I've been hurting him and denying myself. All because I'm afraid."

"Love is scary, and sometimes it doesn't work out, but sometimes it does. Even with Jake's dad, you know. It's worth it. What I mean is, I wouldn't have Jake without what we shared."

Emily's eyes are glassy, and I reach for her hand as she drags me toward her. We hug each other long and hard. "I hope we can keep in touch," she says, giving me a firm squeeze before she releases me.

"We will." I'm fully confident I've made a friend for life.

Still, reality sinks in as I drive away from their house and head for the tannery.

I can't run without letting Dad down. I would have to bring Carter into the tannery and my relationships. While I contemplating how that might work, I spot Skyler's white Durango in the parking lot and let out a breath.

She meets me at the truck door and talks through the rolled-down window. "How'd it go?"

"It was great. Jake's an awesome kid."

"Sorry I missed it." Her salon is generally packed, with appointments nearly always filled a month or more in advance. She'd be making a fortune in tips alone in a big city.

"What are you doing here?" I ask, giving her a onceover and noting she looks ready for a night on the town.

She turns toward her car, then disappears around the side of the building.

After unlocking the back door, I hold it open with my foot and wait for her to return before going inside.

From where I'm standing, something inside the building smells. It's a higher note than the tannery's familiar musty, dead animal scent—a strangely sweet, cloying, chemical smell. I draw in a bigger breath, trying to determine what it is and where it's coming from. I don't even know enough about the tannery to be sure if it's something I should be worried about.

Skyler comes around the building with Mom in tow, whispering about me in an easily discernible tone. I glance between them. Dolled up to the nines. They've been out drinking.

Mom says, "She didn't even invite me."

I didn't invite Mom to attend Jake's day because I didn't want it to be about her. That's what would have happened if she'd been there. Ignoring the rational part of my brain that says Mom's drunk enough that her mood swings are exaggerated, I make an early offensive move and shoot back with, "How's Dad doing?" because she's the only one Dad will let care for him.

"He's so miserable." Her face transforms into a heart-rending look of intense pain. "I have to watch him all the time. He gets these sweats during the night, like chills, until he can't stop shaking. I ask him what he wants, and he's usually just hungry. I've gained fifteen pounds cooking him midnight dinners because he won't eat the food from that book you bought."

When Dad was first diagnosed, I gave her a diet book all about healing MS naturally. I had no idea she took it seriously or cooked meals from it. When she's sober, she refuses to talk about what she does for Dad, saying it takes away from the romance of their relationship and would make me think less of him. It's times like this that Mom is so confusing, making it genuinely hard to be mad at her.

"The first few times he woke up like that, I thought maybe he wet himself, but it's just this disease. He's dying, and I can't do anything to help him," Mom says. Shifting mental gears, she glares at me, poking her finger right in my face. "You're a selfish, terrible daughter, and you're not even looking out for Skyler."

We've been down this road enough times that I know if I take her at her word, going where she leads, I will end up hurt while she won't even remember what she said or did.

Skyler gives me an apologetic look and grabs Mom's shoulders, rubbing her hands down each of her upper arms to soothe her. As screwed as my home life sometimes seems, Skyler's was worse. Still, she always manages to make the best of things, protecting everyone she cares about and caring for Mom in a way I have no patience or tolerance to do.

Going against my better judgment but unable to restrain myself, I ask, "How am I not looking out for Skyler?"

"Don't you think she would have liked to spend a few hours with Max?"

Skyler says, "I'm not interested in Max," but she's just saying that to get Mom off my case.

My phone rings, and seeing Carter's name on the screen, I look at Mom's animated, upset face. "Do you remember asking Carter about his belt?"

"What are you talking about?" Mom asks. "Is Carter calling you?"

"You don't remember, do you?"

Mom turns to Skyler. "Can you believe she asked me that?"

I release the tannery door, shut myself in the truck's cab, and answer his call.

"Hey," I say, sounding like my life isn't a disaster.

"I tried to call you earlier."

"My phone is old and odd when the battery's nearly dead." I plug it into the charger and put the call on speaker.

"How's the accident?" I ask, wondering if it still affects him to see wrecks.

"It's cleaned up."

"Everybody's okay?"

"The driver was texting and ran off the road, but fortunately, she was just slightly banged up. I was thinking about coming to see you. Maybe we could pick up where we left off."

I should be working, but Skyler stands under the tannery's yard light, coaxing Mom toward the car.

When I don't reply, Carter says, "Do you not want to see me?"

"I do. It's just . . ." It felt good to be with him. I don't want to miss out, but I can't miss any more work. "I need to catch up at the tannery, and we agreed to go slow."

"Let me come by. Maybe I can help you catch up."

"I would, but my mom's here with Skyler."

"Then meet me. Just for a minute."

"Okay," I reply because I'd be a fool not to see him again. "Where?"

We meet at the burger joint, buy soft-serve cones, and spend the evening in the back of his truck, laughing and reminiscing about how things went with Jake. When that doesn't seem like enough, he drives out to where we can see the stars, and we sit side by side until I feel like we're getting a whole new chance at what we didn't pursue back then.

I think back on that day at the lake years ago and wonder what would have happened if I hadn't let my feelings get hurt. We might have dated if I had given him the time of day. I could have stayed in Higgins and built a life without feeling I needed to prove myself by moving to New York and pretending to be what I wasn't.

Carter was my crush, the nice guy who cared about me, and at the first opportunity, I pushed him away, convincing myself that he'd taught me a lesson so powerful I never let anyone in. But what if the real problem has been me all along?

I ride the elevator to the neurology department's modern lobby, with muted carpet and pastel paintings, and wait for Dad to come out of his latest appointment.

He still refuses to tell me what's going on with his health, and after listening to Mom last night, I want answers.

The same chipper nurse from last time wheels him into the waiting room.

Dad's steady gaze hits me. "What are you doing here?"

"Just came to see you," I say with a smile. Noting he's got a new wheelchair, I lean in for a closer look. "You got an electric chair?"

"Andrew helped me get it delivered to the house," he replies with a tight smile.

"Wow, that's so nice of him," I reply, equally thrilled and shocked. Maybe Dad's insurance paid for it and Andrew helped get it unloaded.

"I've been meaning to talk to you," Dad says.

"What about?" I ask. Thinking he's going to distract me by talking about dating again, I add, "And don't say you want to know when I'm going on a date with Andrew because I've been seeing Carter almost every day."

"That's what I want to talk to you about." He fixes me with a sad stare.

I feel my brows drawing up along with my shoulders. "Is everything okay?"

"Let's talk about it in the truck." He focuses on the receptionist. In his trademark style, Dad has diverted my attempt to control our conversation.

"I want to know what the doctor said," I reply once he's finished talking to the receptionist.

"That's not what I want to talk about."

My belly knots as I walk down the hall beside his new wheelchair. "Is it about Andrew?" Maybe I owe Andrew an apology for not getting back to him after Dad said I would.

We reach the parking lot and Dad still hasn't replied, but there's a new lift in the bed of his truck.

"You got a lift too," I say awestruck.

"Andrew helped me. Check this out." Dad opens the driver's door and grabs a remote control, then pushes a button that moves the seat out and down. Once it's in place, he positions his wheelchair beside the seat and scoots across. Next, he activates the hoist, positions the wheelchair in the truck bed, and resets the arm in place, securing the chair.

"What do you think?" he asks.

"It's awesome." My voice is chippy. Why did Andrew do this, and how did he afford it?

"Andrew is stable and reliable." Dad's dark eyes pin me in place.

"Did he buy you all this stuff?"

"We traded it for the taxidermy he's having me do. You should see the deer he shot last week."

"How did he afford it?"

"If you talked to him, you'd know he won big prize money in an art show. They're going to put one of his statues at the art museum in Cheyenne."

"That's great." It's a sales pitch, and I'm an uninterested buyer because I have Carter, and he's so right for me.

I'll never forget the wrinkle of Dad's brow or the tightness of his voice when he says, "Carter's not ready to settle down."

"What?"

He looks at me for several seconds before he says, "Charles Corbett stopped by the tannery. He warned me about letting you get involved with Carter. Did you know he's on probation?"

I didn't know, but I concentrate on the words I'm going to say, turning them around in my mind. "I like Carter," I say. "We all make mistakes sometimes, and he's paid the price for his. This might disappoint you, but I really like him."

"Well, then, you decide for yourself," Dad says gruffly.

"That's it?"

He offers me the tiniest smile, then persists in his infuriating meddling. "What do you want me to say? That it's irresponsible to date Carter while he's still living with his grandparents, and they don't approve of him getting involved with you?"

"You wanted me to date Carter." It sounds petulant.

"I'm not insisting you date Andrew," Dad says. "I just want to make sure you're aware."

"I know." His words bear down on me.

"I want my little girl to be happy."

"I am happy."

"I wish you would stop coming to the hospital."

"I wish you would stop trying to get me to date Andrew."

"Watch this." He uses the remote to reposition himself behind the wheel.

I'm truly grateful to Andrew for finding a way to help Dad while letting him do it on his terms. It's not that there's anything wrong with Andrew. Not really. Except he's not Carter. It's unfair to judge Carter the way everyone seems to. He's so good about not judging them.

Dad rolls down his window and motions me closer. "I'm not trying to make you unhappy, Ducky."

"I know." But I'm even less happy than before.

# CHAPTER 16

## CARTER

I PULL up in front of the tannery, bringing Christa back from getting a cup of coffee. I went home and dreamed about her *on our wedding day*. As soon as the sun was up, I invited her to coffee. I'm not desperate to be around her or anything.

She opens the passenger door and puts one foot on the ground before turning to me. "I have to focus on catching up for the next few weeks. If that's not an issue for you, I'd love to see how things go." Her words sound rehearsed, and I know it's an important point for her.

This might sound like a downer, but it's one of the best-case scenarios.

She could have said no. *I don't have time. I don't want to see you.*

I could make an ass out of myself and demand she makes time for me.

Instead, I go for easygoing. Patient. Not exactly the way I'm feeling, but hell . . .

"Of course," I say. "That's understandable. If I want to be in your life, I need to show you that I understand what I'm stepping into."

"Yes," she says. "That's what I need."

"We'll talk." I smile.

She nods then shuts the door.

I watch her walk inside the tannery.

Worried but determined, I tell myself I'm not easily deterred. When I want something, I go all out to get it.

The problem is Christa is like that too. Maybe she knows her dad has the tannery listed for sale. Perhaps they've been arguing about it. I keep thinking I'll ask her, but I'm not sure how she would react to my question, but if things keep going like they are, she's going to burn out and call it off with me. When she does, it's going to burn me down.

I'm thinking about the tannery's newspaper ad and considering calling Leland when Melody pulls up beside me. Leland is in the passenger seat and rolls down his window.

I silence the radio and open the driver's side window. Melody smiles at me politely then turns her attention to Leland. Maybe she doesn't remember?

"Is that the 7.3 liter?" he asks.

"Yeah." I stroke the steering wheel of my new Super Duty. It's a nice truck with the biggest diesel engine they make.

"This year's model?"

"My grandparents bought new trucks for the ranch a few weeks ago."

"Ford's had some trouble with the IPR on those things."

I could pretend to know what he's talking about, but that would be out of character. I stare at the closed door where Christa disappeared. She's slipping away, and I answer his question about the truck with a noncommittal, "She's running great so far."

Leland frowns. "Usually doesn't start acting up so early, but if you notice it stalling or idling hard, check that IPR valve."

"Sure will." As if I'm ever the one to work on my engine. Still, if it would impress Leland, I'd try. I deflect with, "Had any luck with your listing to sell the tannery?"

"You buying?"

"No, sir. I saw the ad in the paper. I'm interested in your daughter, and I've seen her work hard to keep it running. I wondered what might happen."

"Well, the thing is, selling a business like this can take some time. It's a particular industry. Lots of people might be interested, but—"

"No one has called," Melody says. "That's what you're asking, right?"

Leland turns to face her. "You must be patient. It could take six months or more to sell."

"Christa knows?"

"She knows," Leland says, "but she's convinced we can turn it around."

I'm ready to ask why she's convinced when he doesn't seem to be when Leland adds, "She's run one of those retirement calculators they showed her in school or something, and she's decided we'll run out of money if we sell."

"She says I'll spend it all in a month." Melody presses her lips together and looks up at the headliner of their old truck. "As if I would do that when Leland is *dying*."

I refocus on Leland. "You're dying?"

"I'm not dying."

Christa's parents stare at each other. Tears form in Melody's eyes. Leland drags her toward him so she's leaning over the console. She cries harder, with small sobs wracking her chest. He strokes her back gently, and I struggle to understand. Sure, I can tell they're grief-stricken and hurting, and Christa will be devastated, but why keep it from her and let her work herself to death?

"Does Christa know you're this sick?"

They break apart and stare at me. Then as if needing a moment to compose herself, Melody turns toward the opposite window and lets out one more heavy sob before she grabs a handful of tissues from a box in the console.

"I'm not dying," Leland says. "But neither of these women will listen to reason. Did Christa tell you I asked her to stay in New York? Or that I asked her to stop trying to run the tannery?"

Melody chimes in with her two cents, "She doesn't even know what she's doing, trying to run that place like it's not a health hazard."

The tannery's rear door opens, and Christa walks out, eying us.

Leland gives me a pleading look, asking me to understand his reasoning, and I'm not entirely sure I do, but still, it's not my place to step between such a monumental father-daughter situation. I give him a slight nod of ascent, which Christa notes as she steps into the gap between Leland's truck and mine. "What's going on?" When no one answers, she motions between her dad and me, "You two just agreed on something."

"Get over it, Christa," Melody says. "They were talking about Carter's new truck."

"It is a great truck." I feel like a liar even though the words are true.

Christa puts her hand on the window frame and meets my eyes. I stare into her questioning gaze and feel lost, unsure how to make this right. This latest step might lead me down a literal path of doom.

"You better get going," Leland says. "You had somewhere you needed to be."

"Yeah, I've got a thing." I reach for Christa's hand, but she moves away, looking hurt. *Shit. Shit. Shit.*

Attempting to catch her gaze again, I put the truck in reverse.

I finally get a little wave and a forced smile. It feels like failure as I drive toward the ranch, considering asking the grandparents for help—big money kind of help. It might work if I come up with enough money to cover Christa's loans and set up a trust fund for Melody where she can't spend above her means. Christa would be grief-stricken and hurt, but she might turn to me to console her. Maybe we could build a new, *happier* future where we're together.

Sometimes in life I just know things, a gut feeling about what I need to do. It saved my ass a few times while I was in jail, helping me to make friends with the right people. It's one area where Pops and I are alike, and maybe the only trait of his I'd like to inherit. He's seen huge gains, taking the ranch from 40,000 acres to 280,000 acres through solid investing and on the fly decisions to buy out neighboring ranches when someone was in need.

It will take a big step for Christa and me to have a chance at the future I've been imagining. I believe she wants that future too.

I need a buyer for the tannery who's willing to offer what they need, and while the grandparents might be willing to give them a little money, they'd ask all kinds of questions and probably force Christa to keep the tannery open through their need for justification.

Turning around, I head for Jackson to see Abner Jameson, an eccentric guy who went to school with us then started investing in some new kind of currency, NFTs or something like that. We've kept in touch because he's always trying to get me to hunt with him. I've gone a few times, during which he's tried to explain his business to me, but he's impatient, and I get confused by how he jumps around while he talks and distracted because who cares about whatever it is? It sounds like a marketing scheme, convincing you to collect things you don't need.

It's about a three-hour drive to his secure mansion tucked away below the Tetons, and I'll need the time to plan how to convince Abner to buy Leland's tannery.

# CHAPTER 17



## CHRISTA

Just the thought of Carter's hands, the way he seems to know what I need, has my skin tingling and a warm glow washing over me as I wrap up a ten-hour shift at the tannery, finally taking off my flannel overshirt and hanging it on the hook by the door.

Tonight's double date is one more step toward accepting there is a future between Carter and me, which could change everything. It's also a step away from taking Dad's advice, but Dad's worry is based on a conversation with Carter's unreasonable grandfather. Dad doesn't know Carter like I do.

Carter's been to the tannery a few times in the past week, bringing me food and making me take breaks. I told him I implemented new environmentally friendly processes using safer methods, but it's not true. Unfortunately, we have zero money to invest in any of my ideas. It's disheartening, but also the story of my life.

Last to leave the building, I pause at the back door.

The place still smells funny, but I'm unsure what it is. Two of Dad's longtime employees worked with me today and didn't notice it. I'm starting to wonder if my nose is adjusting. Or maybe I'm losing my mind.

Maybe it's only my fear that smells.

My hands are raw, and my hair is brittle from humid chemical-laced air and hide dust. Even after I wash it repeatedly, the smell stays.

I lock up and head home, hoping to have half an hour to spare before Carter is supposed to pick us up.

Another text from Skyler comes through. This one is of her new summer-pink manicure. She started sending messages two hours ago, distracting me with photos of her primping in progress.

She tried to go to California to be near her mom, and she ended up back here, living in a dilapidated trailer, leasing a salon in town.

If I were like Skyler, I'd order a size two when I wear a size four. I'd search the internet for juice fasts, gossip with clients all day, and fantasize about moving to Malibu and shopping boutiques in beachy towns photographed in muted shades of aqua, taupe, and sea foam.

Instead, I'm me. A girl who grew up processing and wearing animal skins, whose legacy may be expanding a tannery and finding a support group so I can learn how to deal with my mom.

Except, there's Carter, asking me to take a chance with him. When I daydream about doing that, I want much more than I've believed possible. I'm all in, but I'm also exhausted and one step away from fucking everything up.

The drive home is short. I walk into our trailer and hear Mom say, "I told Christa to get a new phone. Her battery's always dying."

I pause near the door to listen until I realize there's no vehicle outside. Instead, Mom's voice must be coming over the speaker of Skyler's phone.

"How much did they offer?" Skyler asks.

"They want to look at the books," Dad says.

Could someone have made an offer on the tannery? The prospect seems too good to be true.

Giddy and eager but also afraid of what it would mean to let Dad sell out, let Mom spend the money, let them go broke (if they're going to), and focus on my mess alone, I toss my purse on our lopsided recliner while walking toward the sound. Our threadbare velvet sofa is from the sixties when shag carpet was something people did on purpose. A skimpy, silky red dress is draped across the back, and I run my fingers over the cool, slinky fabric. I'm still touching the couch as I lean into the bathroom. Our place is that small.

"We need to get ready," Skyler says, disconnecting the call. My parents call Skyler to talk instead of talking to me; my presence is enough to make everyone stop talking. It's a new trend bothering me, but I don't have time to focus on that now because Carter will be here in half an hour.

The bathroom is a disaster zone, covered with so much beautification paraphernalia it's almost obscuring the chipped faux tile, press-board embossed with tiny octagons. Skyler's unfazed by the mess and seems ready for a life-altering date.

Her long blond hair is fixed into beachy waves. Her lips are a powdery shade of pink. Her blue eyes sparkle at me behind long lashes, curled and perfect. Her distressed blue jeans and boots are a little too flashy for my taste, but it's a look that works with her long willowy legs.

"We have to hurry." She pouts at me, grabs my hand, and drags me into her place in front of the mirror. "See what I'm up against?"

"Carter has seen me like this countless times." He still likes me. He says I'm beautiful. "What's with the red dress?" I ask.

"Mom brought it for you." Of course, Skyler's mom lives in Malibu, so I know she's talking about my mom.

"I'm not wearing that."

"I know." Skyler squeezes my arm. "I got you something, but let's start with your face."

"Okay," I say with a long sigh.

I close my eyes and let her go to work, trusting her. She knows me well enough to do this and cares enough to do it right. Better than I look now but not over the top or showy.

"Okay," she says, starting to airbrush my skin.

I look in the mirror a few minutes later, and all I can say is, "Wow. You could make so much money."

She gives me a sad, strange look.

"I mean it, Sky. Just because it didn't work out before doesn't mean you couldn't do it."

"Thanks, doll," she says, air kisses me, then checks the timer on her phone. "Eleven minutes. Let's get you dressed. Then we'll touch up your face and do your hair."

I swear she's a miracle worker, and even though I'm not too fond of the tight jeans, the cowgirl top, and how the outfit makes me feel like someone I'm not, I do want to be with Carter, and it doesn't hurt to put out special effort to show it. He's done so much to make me happy.

Not the least was agreeing to and arranging this double date with Max and Skyler. In the back of my mind, I've been trying to give Skyler a chance. I want to help her have one. If only Max can see how sweet she can be. How much she's had to face. How hard she tries. They might be perfect for each other.

Even if he does seem a little cool whenever she's around.

Still, she can be aggressive sometimes. "Maybe take it easy on Max. Women chase him; you might do better taking it easy."

"Easy like: If I could rearrange the alphabet, I'd put U and I together?"

I crack up because, no, that's not what I meant. "Where did you even hear that?"

"A guy said that to me last night."

I don't know how she stands going out the way she does. Even growing up, she had way more charisma and confidence about how other people saw her than I ever did. She knew Max wrote poetry because they were in English class together. So, she copied a poem and then had the guts to read it to him in class. He was either going to humiliate her or take her to the dance. As Skyler finishes curling my hair and fusses over me, I hold my hand to lock fingers. "Pinky swear, we're in this together."

"You're sweet," she says, "but don't let whatever happens with Max and me stop you. You deserve to be so happy."

"I want you to be happy too."

"I am." She locks fingers with me.

The moment lasts a little longer than an easy childlike promise. So long that it starts to feel sad, like she's pretty sure things won't work out with Max. Carter's truck pulls up next to mine in our driveway.

She smiles her beauty queen smile. "I mean it, Christa, don't chicken out."

"I won't," I say it like I'm sure it's true. Surer than I feel. Skyler stays in the hallway while I open the front door and stand before Carter. He's dressed in jeans, boots, and a short sleeve shirt with a collar. So handsome. Just looking at him makes me momentarily stop breathing.

He gives me an intense perusal. "I like your hair."

Instinctively, I pull it over my shoulder. "Skyler did it."

"And you're wearing makeup."

I stand perfectly still. His steady gaze makes me self-conscious. "I am."

I'm also conscious of Carter's proximity and can't help but watch his mouth as it turns up to a small smile, imagining how it would be to kiss him now, my lips against his neatly trimmed beard. I let out a swept-away sigh.

His chest rises and falls as he says, "You look beautiful."

"Thank you," I reply, breathy. "You look good too."

He pulls me forward, drawing me into his arms and making me feel excited, loved, safe, so many things at once. I want this night to be the night. *Our night.*

Sky steps out of the hallway, standing in my line of sight to wink. Carter must feel me stiffen because he pulls away. "Hey, Skyler."

Her decision to come out before we kissed was probably good, given how easy it was to forget she was watching. She sits in the back seat behind me in the truck. He asks her about the salon, and she answers openly, talking about the people who come in, the events around town, and the little old ladies who want their hair a specific shade of blue.

Carter glances over at me with an enduring expression creasing his brow, and I hope Max picks Skyler up the next time we all go out. I hope there is a next time for Skyler because, for once, I feel like the lucky one because of Carter's attention.

A relaxed, contented sort of sound comes with my exhale. As if he can read my mind, he flashes me a smile—not one of the fake I'm-Hot-Shit smiles he offers when he's putting on a show because Carter is one of those guys who knows he makes women swoon, a genuine, I'm-Happy smile. That I've realized the difference and want this one more than anything else shows how far we have come. He lays one hand on the console, and I reach across, taking it in my own.

I'm overcome by a fantastic moment in which I imagine everything standing between us works itself out.

---

The single-story brick building where Max is opening his restaurant is a block from Skyler's salon and flanked on either side by prosperous businesses in two-story structures, with storefronts facing Main Street Higgins and apartments or offices above. On the left is a western boutique, closed for the night. On the other side is a Mexican cantina with a colorful patio and patrons seated and eating, chatting, generally seeming happy to be there.

From the backseat, Skyler puts her hand on my shoulder and squeezes. "You two are so cute together."

A cowboy who looks close to our age, stops Carter in front of the truck to shake his hand and start what looks like it could become a long conversation.

Higgins is a small enough town that our presence at Max's building—entering through the front doors and dressed for a night out—will be circulating gossip within moments. The restaurant isn't open to the public, and there's no sign, but the immaculate exterior has people curious about what's coming. Endless guesses about this latest development will hold a week's relevance. Is the restaurant finally open? Are Skyler and Christa dating Max and Carter? Are they moving the tannery into Max's building? And on and on until the locals develop a story.

People will ask me about it when they see me at the gas pump. If Carter and I don't work out, it will be public information announcement number one, and I'll be dreaming of leaving home again.

He excuses himself, concluding his conversation and coming to my door, holding it open, then closing it behind me before helping Skyler out of the backseat.

"That was Jake's dad," he says, squeezing my hand.

"Really?" I ask. "I thought he was on the circuit."

"He tore his rotator cuff and is home for a while, hoping to work things out with Emily and be around more for Jake."

We enter Max's building through a new vestibule that adds a three-dimensional quality to the storefront and breaks the restaurant's interior from the street outside.

Distracted by this latest development for Jake and Emily, I'm not paying attention to the restaurant and instead ask, "How do you know him?"

"I called him."

Carter didn't really answer my question; still, I'm not sure what to ask first. Is he an asshole? Is he going to hurt them? Should I kick his ass? "Is he . . . ?"

"He's sticking around for a while to see if they can figure it out."

"I hope it works." I really mean it. "But I'm not holding my breath."

"Always the optimist," Skyler says.

"He's not a bad guy." Carter gazes at me earnestly.

"You'll have to fill me in." Maybe it will all work out for the best.

In the dining room, tall brick walls extend to a towering tin ceiling. A partially complete bar covers one wall, turning around a corner near the front to create a natural break in the open room.

A single corner booth sits in the back near a partition wall, concealing the door into the kitchen.

Carter says near my ear, "Max has been trying to finish the dining room for months."

"It looks awesome." It reminds me of New York restaurants with an upscale but relaxed atmosphere. "It's going to be amazing for Higgins."

"Yeah." Carter pauses like he's unsure where to go.

Max comes from the back, emerging from behind the screen wall.

Once he's close, he shakes Carter's hand, exchanging greetings. Carter hands him an envelope.

"What's this?" Max asks.

"Card from the grandparents."

"Hi, Max," Skyler says.

The way Max seems to focus on her gives me hope for the evening.

"Are you going to open your card?" Carter asks.

"Sure, in a minute. But first, let me show you where things are and get you settled."

Max gives us a tour of the restaurant, explaining it's a work in progress, but he has a lot of good ideas and has taken inspiration from restaurants he visited and worked at while attending school in San Diego. His being home makes me wonder if he's a returner like me who didn't make it in a big city despite our best hopes. Maybe he's standoffish because he's had his heart broken.

Skyler's talking to him about her time in Malibu, and Max responds, "Your salon reminds me of something you'd see in a big city." It seems a little forced, but he makes small talk with her, attempting to be interested in Sky's appearance—but he's clearly out of his element talking about hair dye and dry shampoo.

Max is handsome, similar in some ways to Carter, but if it weren't for his clean-shaven face, a person might question his attention to hygiene. "How about we sit?" he says, leading us to a table.

Carter and I settle into the booth beside each other, facing the front windows. Max waits for Skyler to sit before he says, "How about you guys visit while I finish getting everything ready?"

"I can help," Skyler says, scooting off the bench seat and following Max toward the kitchen.

Once they're gone, Carter lets out a heavy sigh. I reach for his hand, and he strokes my thumb like it's the most natural thing in the world that we'd be sitting together in his brother's restaurant —like we've been on a thousand dates, and he knows me well enough to understand I like things like this. "I've been working on ways for us to spend more time together," he says.

"Really?" When would he have time? It seems his schedule is packed between working on his dad's breeding program, cowboying at the ranch, practicing his trick-riding, helping Jake, and visiting me. "What kind of ways?"

"It's a surprise, but I think you'll like it."

We fall into a comfortable silence. It's pleasant to let myself conjure the ways we could find to spend more time together. Unfortunately, nearly all of them require a drastic change to my work/relationship balance and seem too good to be true, reminding me that someone offered to buy the tannery.

It may all work out. Perhaps this whole night will be our fairytale.

A few minutes later, Skyler returns to the dining room and slides into the booth across from us. "The bathroom is so amazing," she says, raising her eyebrows.

Familiar with her escape tactics, I raise one eyebrow.

"Want to see it?" she asks.

I would typically go along with her and head for the ladies to sort out whatever's bothering her, but I trust Carter and want to show it, so instead, I ask, "What's up?"

"Nate." She's twitching her head toward the kitchen like she's been hit with a seizure disorder.

"As in *the* Nate?" Skyler's ex-boyfriend, Restraining Order Nate?

"Yes," she hisses. "In the kitchen. Cooking."

Carter looks between us, seeking an answer from our faces. "Who's Nate?"

Skyler closes her eyes and sucks in a huge breath. A kid playing hide and seek, hoping no one will see her, would look less hilarious.

"He's her ex," I say, hoping to ease the weirdness. Only, knowing Nate is in the kitchen, it's hard. Their history is complicated, involving months of back and forth and ending in restraining orders on both sides.

Skyler opens her eyes wide. "I can't eat anything he cooks. He'll spit in it or something."

"The fuck?" Carter asks, "Why?"

"He hates me."

As uncomfortable as it is, I figure now's as good a time as any to let Carter further into my world. "Last year, Nate was cheating on Skyler and—"

"With my coworker," Skyler adds, sitting up straighter across the table. "A woman I trusted."

"And Skyler was understandably upset."

"When I caught them fucking in my office, I was furious. She hadn't even paid rent in two months."

"To say the least, they were cruel and—"

"Nate is a total dick." Skyler says, "And not in a good way. In an 'I want to castrate you' sort of way."

"Hence the restraining order."

"He has a restraining order against her?" Beneath his beard, Carter's trying not to smile.

Skyler jams her index finger into the table. "Because the justice system is flawed." When neither of us responds, Skyler adds, "He cheated on me."

Her facial expression goes slack, and I turn to see why. Max is headed toward our table, carrying a large platter with an impressive array of dishes. Tense silence settles over our group. How much does Max know about Skyler's breakup with Nate? Maybe nothing. Maybe the whole sordid history.

"It's a small plate menu," Max says by way of introduction as he arranges dishes on the table. He outlines his intended serving order, explaining he'd hoped to show us some of the things he's been working on for the restaurant.

Adorable shortrib sliders. Brazilian cheese popovers with thyme. Chicken on small sticks and paired cocktails for each option.

Max has worked hard to make this happen. I glance at Skyler, wondering how she will play this spread against Nate's presence in the kitchen.

"Is any of this vegan?" she asks.

Max's expression goes slack. "No one told me you were vegan."

"I'm not." Skyler picks up a chicken stick and lays it across her plate before staring at it.

"Your restaurant's amazing," I say, trying not to laugh. "Have you decided what you're going to call it?"

"I was thinking Sterling's. That's what the mercantile that used to be in here was called back when they built the building."

"I think you should call it Max's Grill or something," Skyler says. "With a name like that, people know what kind of food to expect. Plus, everyone around here already calls it Max's Restaurant."

"Yeah. I see what you're saying." He rubs the back of his neck. "But I'm not a fan of restaurants named after the people who started them. I'm hoping for something bigger. Maybe a franchise, eventually."

"What about Ruth's Chris," Skyler says. "They're names."

"Sterling's is a name, too," I add, giving her a look.

"I like Sterling's," he says, then takes a bite of a slider.

Used to getting what she wants from men, Skyler pouts.

I follow Max's lead, going for a slider, figuring Nate wouldn't have done anything too bad if Max was going to eat it too.

"How long has Nate worked for you?" Carter asks.

Max gives his brother a dark look as he finishes chewing. "Why?"

"He's Skyler's ex."

"I know," Max says in a controlled tone.

"Why is he in the kitchen?"

"We're not supposed to be within 300 feet of each other," Skyler chimes in.

"He's not making a big deal out of it."

"You knew?" Skyler asks.

"Nate works for me. It's a small town." Max props his elbows on the table. "I can't choose my employees based on who they've dated."

"But . . ." Skyler's argument peters out. She seems caught between a desire to tell all about Nate and a need to protect her dignity.

"My brother and I need to talk in private," Carter says, standing.

The way they hold each other's stare feels menacing. Carter is tense beside me.

"Fine." Max tosses his napkin on the table, seeming just as dangerous as Carter in his tone and posture.

Our evening has officially turned to shit.

# CHAPTER 18

## CARTER

Pausing to take a breath, I still can't believe what a mad dash this night has been. Wrapping up the last-minute phone call with Abner, only to learn he's expecting something more than a tannery in exchange for his investment, I scrambled to get Christa on time. Now Skyler going bat shit over her ex being here. It's a lot to take in. Let's say I'm a little overwhelmed, but when it comes to Christa, I've got no problem rearranging the world or at least the parts I can control—or, more accurately, attempt to control.

"Is that all?" Max asks after sending Nate home. His voice is dull and monotone.

"He's not coming back?"

"I made him leave after assuring him it would be okay for him to be here while Skyler was here. Why would he ever come back?"

Max picks up where Nate left off, neurotically prepping small dessert cups and plates. I'm not sure how angry he is, but he's a control freak, and everything about tonight is pushing his buttons. We're bothering him when he has a gig. We're invading his restaurant. We're making his crew upset. I just want to get out of here.

"You're still going to drive Skyler home?" I ask.

"You sure that's a good idea?" he says dryly, like the answer's so obvious no man would get it wrong.

I've been using all my leverage to earn a chance with Christa. Should I get Abner to buy the tannery and stress that relationship too? After our last conversation, for which I drove three hours for five minutes face to face, I'm unsure what I'm heading into. Abner has gotten stranger—a bit unhinged even. What if Christa still decides it's best if we're apart? What if she says no?

When I don't respond, Max adds, "Me dating Skyler?"

"Why wouldn't it be?" I lean on the counter next to him.

He focuses his attention on a small jar of candied cherries.

"You could try." I lean into his space to get his attention. "I mean, Skyler's a great girl." From Max's eyebrow twitch, he thinks that's a stretch. "She's attractive," I add. "She's in business like you are. She likes you. It wouldn't be the worst thing for you to have a relationship."

His posture is rigid. He's stressed out all the time. He refuses to give Skyler a chance. I think about the excitement I feel about Christa and wonder why Max wouldn't want that.

"You know . . ." I start to say but stop when he's riveted on his work. "Max." I wait for him to look at me.

There's deadness in his eyes, like he doesn't want to be here. He's had every chance at happiness and is too stubborn to overcome his guilt. White-hot anger flares inside me at the thought of me sitting in jail for him to act like this. I keep my voice even and say, "I gave up a lot for you to be happy."

Something behind Max's eyes seems to flicker and die.

"Right," he says. "That's true, and I'll do whatever I can to make that happen."

He picks up a platter with so much force and combined precision that the gesture comes across as, *Here's your fancy dinner. I hope you choke on it.*

If I could go back and change it all, I probably would because, honestly, did I help Max? I'm not sure I know the answer. "You going to be all right out there?" I ask.

"Yeah," he says through his teeth.

A bitter part of me wants to watch him fall on his ass for being a prick half the time, but he strolls toward the table like a pro.

I've often wondered why my life can't be easier, but being around Max makes me realize how different we are. He's focused on his goals, and the ranch doesn't matter to him, while I've put my life on a slow burner to restore my position at the ranch—becoming Pops's lackey. Maybe Max is happy when I'm not messing with him?

"Nate's gone." I slide in beside Christa as Skyler picks up a fresh drink.

Eight empty glasses are strewn across the table, with only two drinks left untouched. Most of the food is going to be wasted.

Max sets the tray on the table.

"Look at those desserts," Christa says a little too emphatically, sliding a few empty glasses toward our side of the table.

Skyler narrows her eyes at the plates. "I think I gained five pounds looking at them."

Stiff in his dark blue work shirt, Max sits beside her. He couldn't even dress the part or put out any effort to make it seem like he was into Skyler.

Even though the food was decent, I ate zero dinner. I don't enjoy it. Max's mood is stuck to me like a burr, festering and grating against my last frayed nerve. I'm annoyed with Max's attitude, but really, I'm annoyed with myself. I should never have asked him to do this, but I'm unsure how to fix it.

I want to get out of here, so it's a relief when Christa says, "Maybe we should clean up since Max cooked us a delicious dinner."

"Glad you liked it, but I can clean up." He smiles at Christa.

"We can take Skyler home," I offer because I'm not that much of an asshole.

"I'll do it." He might as well be a corpse for how energetic he seems, but he does what he's promised, letting Christa and I take off while Skyler stays to help him clean up.

As soon as we're outside, I pull Christa toward me on the sidewalk, not caring that people on the adjacent patio might see. Under the streetlights, with flyaway hair and a sparkle in her eyes, she looks more alluring than ever, or maybe it's how good she makes me feel.

"What do you want to do now?" she asks.

"That's all I got," I say in mock seriousness.

She gives me an unreadable look, then says, "I wish we'd spent the night on our own."

"We still can." Having spent time thinking about where I'd take her, someplace private but where I've never taken another woman, I've figured this out. "Let's go for a drive."

Once we're in the truck and headed toward the ranch, she asks, "Is everything okay between you and your brother?"

"Yeah," I say too quickly.

"I'm sorry I made things harder for you by insisting on a double date."

"It's no big deal." I turn the radio on.

"I think it's sexy that you can play the guitar, and your singing voice is pretty amazing," she says, making me shy in a way I haven't felt since boyhood.

No one has ever taken my singing or playing seriously; she seems to mean it. Something heavy inside me shifts. If I watch her a second longer, I may run us off the road, but I don't want to lose the odd mixture of satisfaction and gratefulness she's inspired. It's like she's given me a precious gift I want to hold onto.

I drive toward the place I've prepared for us and turn down a hardly discernible road. The headlights illuminate sagebrush, and the truck bumps over ruts and rocks.

"Is this safe?" she asks.

"I've been down this road a thousand times. My pheasant blind's up here." Along with a pond and an old barn. If the night goes well, we could end up on a blanket in the hayloft.

Oddly, the abandoned buildings used to make me sad, like life would pass me by if I didn't figure out a path forward.

Now, I pull up beside the barn, full of anticipation about a future unfolding into what might make for a great life.

I shut off the truck and walk around to open Christa's door.

She doesn't move at first, looking at me like she's unsure of our next step.

"We don't have to do anything but look at the stars or talk or whatever you want to do," I say, meaning it.

"Whatever I want?" A coy smile grows on her lips.

"Whatever you want." I trace a finger around her ear, touching her soft hair and eliciting sweet sounds of pleasure.

"Let's sit in the back," she says.

I grab a blanket from the backseat, spreading it across the bed, then we climb in. I sit, leaning against the toolbox, then pull her toward me so she sits with her back pressed against my front.

We discuss Jake, his dad, Colt Foster, former Saddle Bronc Champion, and Emily. I fill her in on our plans to get Jake riding, then tell her how special she is for wanting to help that family and how I'd like to create my own family with her.

She's lighthearted, laying her head on my shoulder. "We'll have a boy smarter than me who can demolish all your rodeo records."

"Is that what you want?" I ask, profound as a deathbed prayer.

"Do you think you might want to marry me? Not now, I mean, someday?"

"I'd marry you tonight."

She gazes at me for a long moment until she looks away, gazing past me, like she realizes she took the conversation in the wrong direction and isn't sure how to take the words back.

I remember her saying we should take it slow.

Even though I'm just as unsure how to slow down, I wonder if she still thinks what's going on between us needs to be reined in. It seems fast, but it feels right, maybe because of how long we've cared about each other. I start to ask how she feels, knowing all the reasons she's explained. Stopping me, she presses her lips to mine, and it's a sweet kiss that turns into more. I like us like this, exploring and tentative rather than hot and frantic.

This kiss feels like we're building something important like she's still that girl who knew what I needed when it seemed no one else did. I want to be that person for her and break away, feeling like I have important things to say before we go further, talking about marriage or kids.

"Christa," I say her name in a low voice, making her look at me. "There are some things I need to tell you."

# CHAPTER 19

## CHRISTA

MY WHOLE MIDDLE freezes at Carter's words, *There are some things I need to tell you.* His earnest tone makes me certain he will say critical somethings and reminds me of Dad's warning about Carter not being ready to have a relationship. *Did you know he's on probation?*

Carter reaches for my hand, bringing my fingers to his lips. The torment of not knowing what he wants to say is almost unbearable.

Then he places my fingers delicately on the blanket.

He shakes his head, resetting himself, then speaks. "There are things you should know. It won't change anything between us, or at least, I hope it won't, because when I look at you, I think this is it."

He pauses, studying me, waiting for that to sink in, then says, "I see my whole future with you, but I don't think it's fair of me not to tell you. I should have already told you . . . You can still change your mind about us."

"Okay." Maybe my tight chest will eventually release and let me breathe.

"There's a civil judgment against me for restitution because of the criminal case against me. It's half a million dollars, but I don't intend to pay it. Still, my credit's wrecked, and I don't have access to money like you might think. I don't have a house."

"Okay." He's on probation. He's worse off financially than I am. Dad already mentioned he lives with his grandparents. But this judgment is new. "What happens if you don't pay the judgment?"

Coyotes start-up, carrying on an eerie conversation, that crosses miles of his family's land.

"Nothing, really. It's a civil action. If I get a job, they'll garnish my pay. Just makes things harder." Carter shifts away from me and gazes at the horizon. I know him well enough to understand this isn't easy for him to admit. All his life, he's known he was destined for a specific life on their ranch, only to have his dreams stripped away.

Even though, in some ways, he's had a more privileged life than me, he's had a hard life. One that's left him scarred and burdened. He may not be Prince Charming, riding in to rescue me and move me into his palace, but he's genuine, loyal, and honest, and I love him for making me laugh, feel, and desire something more. So, I lean into him and wait for him to look at me. "I want to be with you. We can work it out. Money doesn't matter." Only it does matter. Immensely.

"I have a plan," he says. "As long as you trust me, we'll get it all. Everything will work out."

"Okay." Even as I say it, I feel a little sick at how we can make it work. "I trust you."

"I like hearing you say that." His lips tip into a smile.

And with him baring himself so earnestly, I know I should

offer him a little of my embarrassing history, only I'm not sure I've got the courage. Still, it took a lot for him to trust me.

I lean toward him and lay my head on his muscular shoulder, inhaling his aftershave, realizing I shared the truth about the tannery early on. He's kept my secrets and tried to help. This is a chance at something with Carter, and I want that chance.

To cement that fact, I add, "I got arrested in Ithaca a few months ago."

"Yeah?" His voice is a little awed as he tilts his head to look down at me.

I lift one shoulder. "Did you think I was an angel?"

"Pretty much are." He traces a finger down the curve of my neck, making me realize he might not ask me why I went to jail.

He circles his finger, tracing a pattern up my neck again before it dips under the neckline of my shirt, teasing gentle touches, sending a current of desire through my limbs, making me want more.

I shift forward to see him and gaze into his gray eyes. "You're not going to ask me why they arrested me?"

He leans in, his chest pressed to mine. He breathes close to my mouth, making me remember how he tastes. I want to kiss him again.

"Darlin'," he says, hitting me with the full heat of his charm, "do you want to tell me about it?"

My past is so irrelevant in light of what he's been through, it seems almost silly to dwell on it, so I whisper, "I'd rather do this," and I kiss him.

And kissing Carter is hot. His beard is just right, and his hands twining in my hair are urgent but gentle, like he under-stands what it will take to make me feel unimaginable pleasure. Seeming to read my mind, he deepens the kiss, levering against me until I moan into his mouth.

He pulls back just enough to whisper, "Jesus, darlin'," before he shifts forward, kissing me hard, wedging me against his toolbox as I pull him in.

I want this, and I move against him, my heart pounding as I shift until my hands are on his shoulder, allowing me to push up to my knees.

His hands loop around my waist, pulling me forward as he drops his mouth to mine, sending heat coursing through me in an even more powerful surge of lust. Fuck me.

And I want to fuck him.

We're getting carried away. I know there could be a future for us together, but there's still a lot I'm responsible for. And I can't abandon all that. I can't spend time out with Carter all the time and not ruin everything else.

He breaks our kiss and sits back a few inches, not fully stopping but testing the situation as he studies me and asks, "You okay?"

"Yeah." It sounds high and fake.

"All right." He sits back.

"I want to. Sorry . . ."

He lifts one eyebrow and half-smiles. "You're apologizing for that?"

"I mean—"

"No." He shakes his head. "You can't."

"Okay." I smile, glad about the shift in our mood. Carter's so good at reading what I need.

He reaches for my hand and twines our fingers. "Tell me what you're thinking."

I like how our joined hands feel and focus on his solid grip as I gaze at him. "This is fun, and we're having fun, and I like it a lot, but . . . It's hard to be away from the tannery. I have a lot to do right now, and I'm not sure how we'll make it all work. I get so focused on this, I mean us, that I'm not paying attention to other important things."

"Okay," he says.

"But when you say stuff like 'I'd marry you tonight,' it scares me. Like you want to go faster."

"Oh. Okay." Carter regards me for a while, and I gaze back at him in the full moon's light. Noting the worry line between his eyebrows, I blame myself. I'm still a mess of desire and fear.

I don't want to push him away, so I reach up and kiss him, wanting to share how I'm feeling. "It's scary to think of marrying, isn't it?"

"I don't mean to scare you." From his earnest tone, I know I've hurt his feelings and I hate myself for that.

"I was the one talking about having kids," I admit.

"But that was before you knew what a wreck my life was."

I gaze at him and realize that's true. I said it didn't matter, but here I am, proving myself a liar.

"Maybe we should . . ." I start to say, then stop. I don't know what to do. And that's the problem, I'm talking and acting like I have answers, but I don't.

Tomorrow. I will think about it tomorrow—first thing in the morning because I'm resting with my cheek on Carter's cotton shirt.

His arm drifts up to my chin, tilting it with his fingers until our gazes lock. "I can hear you thinking."

One second, I'm nosediving into worry. The next, I'm caught in his loving and earnest gaze. Without hesitation, I lean into him. He reciprocates, cradling me close to his chest. His steady heart beats with calming reassurance.

"Want to talk about it?" he asks.

His sultry voice and the tender, patient way he's waiting say we can talk all night, but this choice is too big. Letting Carter know why I'm nervous would mean unpacking Dad's warning, and I want Carter despite his past, so I whisper, "I don't want to think about it."

With him focused on me, everything else in the world goes out of focus, but my mind won't stop. Is all this passion love or lust? I'm clearly out of my mind. After all the times he's told me we should take it slow, I want to claim him like we're meant to be—like he will vanish at midnight if I don't do the right things to make him stay.

"Stop worrying." His voice is rough against my ear. "Please, just stop."

His fingers stroke my neck, and I lose myself in the sensation of his lightly calloused fingers working so earnestly to please me. "Please keep doing that."

"This?" He nuzzles my neck. "Or this?" His mouth moves lower over the collar of my top while he palms my left breast. A hot trail of sexual desire traces through my stomach, gathering in my throat until it escapes as a moan.

His hands run down my body, grasping me by the hips and pulling me toward him. "We can just do this," he says against my neck.

"And see where it goes." I lean into his touch.

"Maybe I should tell you more of my secrets." Carter nips at my ear.

"And I'll tell you the rest of mine," I whisper.

And making out with him like this is fun. He knows I need time, and we're on the same page, trying to figure this out.

I brush the hair at his collar, wanting to make sure we figure it out.

His expression is tender, thoughtful, and full of adoration when he says, "I want to show you this isn't a passing thing for me."

# CHAPTER 20

## CARTER

EVEN MY DOGS seem to notice I'm distracted because instead of following me, Job and Kim lounge under a shade tree and leave me to work in the hot July sun. I've been up since before dawn, managing the rotation of horses for our equine vet as their team examines our mares. Normally, I live for this shit—taking notes, analyzing data, and preparing production plans. But today, my mind is on Christa, what she's doing right now, what she's thinking, does she regret last night, or is she reliving it and waiting until the next time we touch? My mind's wanderings are . . . not excessive, but intense and more attention than I've ever given another person. I've always put the ranch first.

By noon, I've had enough of the vet visit and am ready to forget about Dad's quarter horse brand for a while. I strip off my shirt, reach into my pickup for a towel, wipe myself down, and put on a fresh shirt. Then, I drive to where the vet's working and talk through the rolled-down window like an asshole, leaving them to wrangle things, making an excuse about needing to go, promising I'll follow up in the next few days for a report.

I drive out of West Creek and contemplate my life—one where a dream I've held onto for so many years is now secondary to a new plan.

I have found a woman like the one I've been praying God would send. I've never let anyone own me like Christa does. Hell, until now, only preserving Dad's legacy has ruled me like this.

The idea of forming a family with Christa is more potent than anything I've ever dreamed of.

My hand fists around the steering wheel. My knuckles are white. Half of me wants to slow down, but I love her, and she loves me back. She trusts me. The only acceptable course of action is to prepare for our life together.

I outline my goals: get the tannery sold, find someplace to live, and convince Nonna to give me one of the Corbett rings. Once I have those things in place, we can think about what's next. It will take time to accomplish, so I start right away, calling Max to implement step one: Get Max on my side.

When he doesn't answer, I leave a message. "Call me when you have a chance. It's important." I regret how we left things last night. Still, maybe his night turned out alright after all. Skyler wasn't home when I dropped Christa off.

I call Abner next to meet up with him about finalizing the tannery paperwork. When he answers, he asks, "Did you see my texts?"

"Not yet. What is it?"

"Read them."

"I'm driving. Tell me."

"An address, but don't put it in your phone. Read it all. And follow the directions. Exactly as written."

"Okay."

"Take this seriously."

He's gotten more annoying. "What's your concern?"

"Don't ask stupid questions."

"How is that a stupid question?"

"Don't fuck this up."

This guy has zero patience, and while typically I negotiate from a position of power, I need his help. Christa needs his help, and I'll be his stooge for her.

"Have you spoken to Leland?" I ask.

"My attorney did."

"You're not going to tell me where you left things?"

"Stop stalling and get here."

"Where?" I ask, driving west toward Jackson.

"Read the messages." Abner ends the call.

Pulling over, I check my phone, nine texts. The most ominous one says, "you'll know it when you see it." There's no address, only an explicit directive: *Do not use turn-by-turn directions.*

I need to get to Ballford, Wyoming, population one. It's a ghost town so far south it's almost to Colorado. No one goes to Ballford as a destination. No one.

A bitter taste coats my tongue. Probably because I haven't eaten since before dawn, not because I have zero control over how this unfolds or because Abner knows I need him much more than he needs me. I'm lying to myself, and I hate that almost as much as I hate knowing Christa is stuck at the tannery.

I turn the truck around and head southeast to pick up I-80, half expecting my destination to be a bunker-like structure similar to Abner's house in Jackson, concealed by tall walls. Or maybe it's a private golf oasis on the plains or a decommissioned missile silo—a fallout shelter, the stuff of a prepper's wet dreams.

Maybe I should have brushed up on my survival skills or packed water and weapons. It's one of a thousand possible scenarios, none of which eases my grating nerves.

Three and a half hours later, I'm almost to Ballford. I've exercised my imagination and failed to distract myself from the festering, annoying powerlessness.

I pass the lone business in town, a trading post selling gas, and turn north, following the instructions even though I'm almost sure there was a shorter, faster way to get there.

The road continues past a series of low draws toward the horizon. Over the subsequent rise on the left is a half-complete structure. It looks like a house stacked on top of a house, with another smaller house on top and so on, all the way up to a set of timbers waiting for something else that hasn't yet been installed. It's Abner's weird. He would build a house that most men would be afraid to enter and make me drive here without explanation.

He's sick and twisted like that.

I pull through the open gates, made of twelve-by-twelve timbers, and park next to his truck, surprised it's the only vehicle here and half expecting he's got an airfield out here given his pilot's license and love of jets with short runway, high-altitude performance.

Even if he is rich, he spends too much. It won't surprise me if he turns up broke. Just not now. Please, not now.

He walks out of the house wearing a golf shirt, slacks, and shiny shoes.

I won't apologize for my boots and jeans. "What've you got going on here?" I ask by way of greeting.

"Tower house," he says and goes on and on about it going up as high as possible and how he's disappointed about stopping at two hundred feet because federal airspace begins, restricting any further building. He's one of those guys who shaves his head to a military cut even though he's not enlisted or balding. Finicky. Eccentric. Emotional.

Somewhere in the first five minutes, I realize he brought me here because he's lonely, wanting me to pal around with him. I'm in if touring his hobbit house is what it takes to get Christa's tannery sold.

"A friend of mine lives in a converted water tower," he says when I ask him where he got the idea.

"You put in an airfield?" I ask, not seeing one.

"You have to see the cave," he says, giddy as I've ever seen him.

"What cave?" I ask dryly.

"Come on," he says. "Follow me."

I wouldn't say I like caves. Dark places. All confined places. Never have. Don't ask me why. I couldn't say except that it intensified during my firefighter training. We learned about the problems with air in places like that—oxygen-deficient atmospheres. Just thinking about it, my chest gets tight.

Abner turns, giving me a side-eye. "Tell me you're not afraid of bats."

"Nope," I reply. "Couldn't give a shit about bats."

He leads me into the house. The atrium is open to the sky. Once it's complete, with a structure above, I imagine it going all the way up. Twenty stories. The sort of place where a kid could wreak havoc, dropping things from above.

He grasps the doorknob on a hewn wood door and pauses, looking at me expectantly. I can only guess he's hoping to build suspense.

I shrug.

He opens the door and reveals a mine shaft that drops into the earth. After ten feet, it's all dark.

"Want to go in?"

No way in hell. "I have to get back."

He deflates, running a hand over his buzzed head, then, "You're a pretty good shot, aren't you? You were when we were kids."

"I guess."

"It's not a big deal," he says, shutting the door on the mine and heading up the staircase. He grabs a beautiful bolt-action 30.06 with a figured walnut stock from the second landing, then continues until he stops at the highest level. It's a floor three stories in the air with structural timbers and the surrounding walls incomplete.

He brings the rifle up, aims, fires—at what I'm not sure—then: "I want you to settle a deal for me," he says, handing me the rifle.

Wondering about the target, I sight through the scope. "Why can't you do it?"

It's annoying when he ignores me, leaving me staring through the scope.

"Keep looking, and you'll figure it out," Abner says.

I scan the open green of high-altitude summer grass, spotting soft gray stone, delicate arroyos, and elk while seeking something Abner's brand of weird. About 300 yards away, an array of muted white golf balls stand out, but it's likely his latest attempt at golf. Beyond sits a stone portico. Inside are stacked skulls and bones, with oxidized antlers, all piled into an eerie monument like a burial ground in an old Western. Someone's heredity, left to rot. Sun and wind testing its edges.

When we were kids, we went up in the gold mines on the ranch, where no one goes, and found ancient human skeletons in the ore piled at the end of a timber sluice.

I lean the rifle across my shoulder.

"Too creepy for you." He grins, toothy and amused.

"Some things you just don't do," I reply, remembering what we did with the bones back then and never feeling right about it.

I hand him the rifle and turn toward the steps. "How about you tell me why I'm out here."

"Fine." He slings the rifle over his shoulder. "I've funded an LLC. You finish the deal. Sign the papers today."

"And that's it?"

He shrugs. Coy and manipulative. What a weasel.

"Abner."

"I buy the tannery with a phone call. We both walk away with what we want. Plus, I get a new business in my old hometown."

I don't like it, but say, "What's the risk?"

Abner leans out over the edge with no railing, gazing down, making me want to grab his arm and pull him back. "Remember how scared we all were of Leland back in the day?"

"I'm still scared of him." It's true, because even though Leland isn't the force he once was, Christa loves him. She respects him.

"He owns a business perfectly suited for dismemberment and disposal of evidence," Abner says, making my blood run cold even though the tannery only handles hides. He's just being an asshole, though, trying to get me worked up.

"You know you're talking like a freak?" I ask, channeling Max, asking a question no sane man would get wrong. I stare at Abner, his thin face and pasty white skin. I wait for him to respond.

"With your family name, no one will question it."

"Question what? What are you buying? Or should I ask, what am I buying?" *And why?*

I start to feel physically ill, both from the height and the situation unfolding, mainly because of what it means if I don't go through with it. Christa will be stuck at the tannery. What choice do I have? Rules are less critical when I'm helping those I love.

My phone rings. It's Max calling me back.

"It's Max," I tell Abner.

"I'll get the notary," he says to my back.

I wander down the stairs without answering the call. Maybe it annoys Abner that I'm walking away now, but I'm tired of playing pattycakes. I want to get in my truck and drive.

I wish I'd never come. I wish I had just moved on after I got out of jail. Forgot about Dad's legacy. Forgot about the ranch and the family name, pride, and loyalty. What does any of it matter when no one else cares? I could start over fresh and build a life of my own creation.

The phone rings. I answer and start implementing my plan,

because when a person is this far down a track, it's hard, if not impossible, to turn back.

I tell my little brother about Christa. My dogs love her. She's the one. I segue into the importance of independence. *We* need independence. I emphasize we, even though he's already carved out the slice of life he wants.

"Why not take a few more rooms at the main house?" Max asks.

It's what I've always wanted to do, but I expand on all the reasons independence is essential. Escape the grandparents' watchful eye, move on from the past, find some privacy, and start a family. I wrap up my long sermon with, "Hell, I may even get along better with Pops and Nonna. It all makes sense." Even as my stomach twists into knots.

"I get it." His voice is earnest, and I believe he does.

Silence lingers between us—my neck prickles. Abner's standing in the doorway. Has he been listening?

"What if we pay off the judgment?" Max asks. "Probation's almost over. You could move on with your life."

*Where would we get the money?* He knows I'm thinking it because he says, "The grandparents gave me a check in that card you brought the other night."

"How much?" They wrote me a check for five grand on my last birthday.

"Enough to pay off your judgment."

"Five hundred grand?"

"It was like a homestead grant they announced at Jake's wish day, except they said it wasn't like that. They didn't want us to apply for the program. They didn't expect us to, but I did, and they gave me the money. They said to spend it on a dining room for Sterling's, but what if . . . I was thinking . . ."

He rambles on and on about how bad he feels about hurting the guy. He wishes he'd never done it. He wakes up sweating in the night, afraid of his temper. He's fucked up. It's all about him.

"I'm not paying the drunk driver who killed our parents a

goddamned shiny nickel," I say through gritted teeth. "You understand?"

"But—" Max starts to argue.

I cut him off. "Want to fix things between us?"

"Of course."

"Keep half of it. Give me the rest."

Remembering Abner, I glance up.

He's standing in the doorway with a notary. "We're ready for you," he says.

"I gotta go," I tell Max, "but that's the deal. You do this, the past is in the past. Forgotten. I won't bring it up ever again."

It's not how I saw the conversation going, but I hang up the phone, thinking about how far I can get on a house for two hundred and fifty grand.

Then I walk inside the crazy tower and ask as many questions as possible about the deal I'm about to make with the devil.

Abner's notary—a young blonde woman in tight jeans—lays the pages out before me. Apologizing for keeping her waiting, I read every word.

"You don't have to read it," Abner says when I'm halfway through the fifty or so pages.

Most of it's boilerplate, legalese, and maybe he's right, but still, I don't trust easily, and I'm not signing anything until I know what it means. Reaching the last page, the deal seems innocent enough, some land just like Abner said, until I zero in on the final exhibit, a legal description that seems oddly familiar. I pull out my phone and navigate to a web page, mapping township and range. The parcel is adjacent to West Creek's boundary near Echo Canyon. Near the abandoned gold mines where, as adolescents, we spent endless summers doing things we shouldn't have.

"Abner,"—I control my voice and concentrate on flipping the papers back to the front—"why didn't you tell me this deal was right next to West Creek?" When he doesn't respond, my anger builds until I can't hold it inside. "You didn't think I would understand it, did you?"

A mirthless smile creeps over Abner's face. Then he laughs, a devilish little chuckle. "You're still going to sign it, aren't you?"

What would Abner want with land adjacent to ours except to mine it? Develop it? Resorts. Subdivisions. Doing damage worse than the grandparents' homesteaders.

I choke on my next breath. The air that should be coming in and out of my lungs has gotten caught somewhere in between.

If I sign this, I'll be selling my soul for a chance in heaven.

Maybe I'll get in.

# CHAPTER 21

## CHRISTA

ALL I WANT IS to be with Carter.

So what if both of us have financial problems and odd family dynamics? It seems we're two of a kind, and the similarities are so painful it's almost laughable.

"Just take it easy," Carter said when he dropped me off last night. "Everything's going to be okay. Just trust me."

But I don't want him to carry my burdens. I definitely won't let him try to do it alone.

I'm anxious and jittery about needing to fix things on my end so we can move on to bigger and better things. Together. I don't want to lose him.

I've been trying to find out who the prospective buyer is, and after learning from Dad that he didn't even get a phone number so he could follow up, I'm not convinced it will happen. The buyers haven't called. No one has looked at the tannery or reviewed our books. It takes months or even years to sell a business.

I'll convince some sad soul that our tannery is the deal of a lifetime, but I'll never get the price Dad wants given the state of our building and books. We have a compelling history and a sizable customer base, but we're not flourishing. Prices will have to go up, and is Dad right that if we raise prices, customers will go elsewhere?

Before dawn, I pull up behind the tannery.

Near the back door, illuminated by the security light, are four silver chemical drums. Our delivery came while no one was here to receive it, and the driver left it near the door. Add that to my list of things to do. I'm at my desk, setting down my things, and my coffee cup leaves a puddle. I pick it up and gulp, but a crack circles my favorite mug.

*Coffee.* I salvage what I can into a fresh mug in the small break area. This one has a cat giving the middle finger and saying, "I do what I want," making me grin. Not that I do what I want, but still, I can have a sense of humor.

I set the coffee on my desk and get the pallet jack, maneuvering the first drum through the roll-up door. It has a bit of corrosion around the bottom. I need to ask Dad what we should do.

Back at my desk, I can't find my phone. I'm the one who canceled the landlines to save money after forwarding all the calls to Dad's mobile since he's rarely here anymore. Who do I blame that I can't call him? My computer chimes, notifying me about several new messages. I open my email— customer inquiries waiting for responses, regulatory reminders, and a notice from our insurance agent.

I spend an hour returning customer messages, then write to my college mentor, asking him to assess the value. I re-read what I've written and hit send.

Still unable to find my phone, I start in, adding hides to the tanning drum, flipping the switch to turn it on. Rhythmic pounding follows me out of the room. In the hanging room, I check the hides and adjust the heaters before returning to the storeroom to deal with the leaky delivery. Unfortunately, more liquid has leaked out, seeping between the old wooden planks into the basement below, soaked with years of chemicals and oils.

I pull the packing list out of the stick-on label. The delivery is addressed to our neighboring co-op.

Maybe fertilizer.

Shit. Shit. Shit.

I should have looked at this before I moved it inside.

The cowbell hanging from the front door handle rings.

I pile the rags in the corner and head out to meet whoever's there.

Skyler says, "Hey, girl."

I bite my tongue against asking her to leave. "Can it wait until I get home?"

She pouts. "I want to know . . . How was last night?"

I heave out an exasperated sigh and evade. "Where were you?"

"I stayed out in case you came home and wanted privacy."

"With Max?"

She drops her voice and puffs up her chest to mimic him. "I don't do relationships. It's not you. It's me. I don't want to hurt you."

"It sounds like maybe it's the truth."

"But I love him." She's breathy and laughing.

"Stop doing that. It's annoying."

She shoves papers aside and plants herself on the corner of Dad's desk. The one that's become mine. "You're grumpy. Last night was bad?"

"No, it was great." I scrape a hand through my hair.

"Okay."

I glance at the boxed hides I plan to get through before I leave. "I don't have time to talk about it right now."

"Fine."

Silence settles between us, and finally, I feel bad and say, "Thank you for staying out to give me a chance with Carter. Everything with him is amazing."

"He is so into you."

And I feel so lucky about that. "I'm sorry it didn't work out with Max."

Skyler raises her eyebrows and grins. "I have a date up in Jackson tomorrow night." She drones on about this latest guy. He's right up her alley. He skis. He's rich. He's handsome. I should see his profile. He has a condo right in the resort. And on and on.

Thinking I've fulfilled my social obligation, I focus on the computer, half listening until I refresh my inbox and stop paying attention altogether to focus on the response from my former professor.

He's glad to hear from me. He hopes my father's doing well. He answers my question with a list of businesses he's seen sell. Numbers that are all over the place. I can only interpret them to mean annual revenue is typically more than the selling price. Since our gains have been negative for the past few years, it bodes poorly for us.

And he goes on . . . Reading between the lines: Selling the tannery is going to cost us more than we'd make.

I interrupt Skyler. "You need to go." Realizing how it sounded, I soften the command. "Okay?"

I'm sure she's got an appointment coming up anyway. She leaves without fussing, never sticking around for more than half an hour.

Who would want to? I glance around at the building, the chemical tanks, and the outdated equipment—dust coats nearly every surface. Even the light bulbs are mostly burned out. Like so many small family-run businesses, this place is worth hardly anything.

We have to raise prices. Even if Dad says it will run

customers off. We have to do something. Or I have to leave. Go out on my own. Get a job. Survive without worrying about their circumstances.

My phone dings and I grab it from under a pile of papers, realizing too late the battery has hardly any life left as I read Emily's text.

> Emily: How are things with Carter?

I'm suddenly overcome by the hyper-aware yet helpless feeling I had the night I learned Dad was sick.

Emily's text has sent me down yet another circular trail. We text back and forth for a few minutes, me telling her we're taking things slow so I can focus on work, her filling me in on Colt's reappearance in Jake's life.

As happy as I am for them, I close out our messages and check on the batch of hides I started earlier, then unpack our latest deliveries, which arrive salted and need to be started in the large square liming vats to soften and prepare the hides for tanning. More hours run off as I sit behind the sanding machine finishing hides that are further ahead in the process.

I don't want to let Carter go. That's the problem. What I have with Carter is real. I want to see it through. Fear grows from a seed in my mind into a knot in my stomach. It's going to be hard, but I don't let it get me down because deep inside, I know I'm going to make it through alright. I give myself a pep talk. *Bring it on.*

Finishing seventeen hides leaves me pleased.

But a genuinely odd smell hangs in the air, stranger, more metallic than normal. Maybe it's electrical?

Behind me, the air changes pressure.

A whispered hiss.

In biology class, I learned humans have primal survival mechanisms that remain from our days as cave dwellers in constant threat of danger. There may be something to it because as the air moves, my ears ring.

What happens next takes half a second at most.

A whoosh of air makes me weightless, flinging me forward. My knees and palms smack the floor. A tremendous boom reverberates, shaking the tannery's walls and sending high-speed debris into the air.

# CHAPTER 22

## CARTER

I WAITED AROUND for Abner's attorney to put together a purchase agreement for the tannery and watched Abner sign it digitally and email Leland a copy. He deposited fifty thousand into escrow as earnest money and is waiting for Leland to respond, signing his side or countering the offer.

That's progress for a day. Lots of people would be satisfied, but I want more.

Nearly all my life, I've heard about the Corbett rings. Growing up, the stories were annoying, old-fashioned, and embarrassing for my forefathers, who always seemed too desperate to be authentic. One ordered a bride by stagecoach, and another fell in love with a forbidden princess, but the older I got, I was glad to have the family history and the knowledge that one day, when I found the right woman, I wouldn't have to go searching for the right ring. All I had to do was tell the grand-parents, and they would let me choose.

I've never seen the rings, and I'm not sure of much, but I'm pretty sure Christa will love the stories behind them. *Pretty sure.*

Pretty sure of this. Pretty sure of that. I've got a lot on the line right now, like I told her. All my cards are on the table. If she can have a little patience and trust me, it's all going to work out.

I roll the window down and tell myself everything is going to be okay. The truck roars down the dusty county road with the sun dipping below the horizon as I'm pulling through the ranch's main gates.

As soon as I get home, I approach Nonna in her garden. She's on her knees in a strawberry bed, and when she sees me, she smiles.

Might as well jump in headfirst, except my words don't seem to come. My hands are shaking. I kneel beside her and focus on a dandelion, gripping it just right to avoid tearing off the leaves. I pull a few more weeds, allowing myself to relax for a few minutes.

"What's on your mind?" Nonna asks, side-eyeing me, and I get it. Under normal circumstances, I wouldn't join her in the garden or pull weeds.

No sense lingering. I lay it all on the line, explaining my connection with Christa. Somewhere along the way, I resume pulling weeds. Nonna's a good listener. She doesn't interrupt as I talk about how special Christa is, how I'd like to have a future with her and ask her to be my wife.

"Do you love her?" Nonna raises her eyebrows. As expected, she seems happy I'm taking a step forward with my life. For a long time, she's prodded me to notice every female in my vicinity as a prospective wife.

"Yeah." A smile breaks over my face. I imagine Christa the way she was last night, lying on my chest, making me feel complete. "I do."

"Let's look at the rings." Nonna strips off her gardening gloves and stands.

I follow her into a large, windowed study attached to one end of her and Pops's bedroom. While she goes to open the safe, I sit, trying to relax but feeling just as rigid as the stiff-backed antique sofa I'm leaning against. I look across the hay fields toward the mountains and feel hopeful about all of it.

One day, in the not-too-distant future, this land will welcome me as the owner—a trusted steward to protect her tradition and wilderness.

Nonna comes back, carrying a shiny wooden box. "I should get your grandfather," she says, setting it on the table.

Unease presses around me. "Do we have to?"

"Well, eventually, you'll have to tell him. Let me call him on the intercom."

While Nonna presses a button on the wall and talks to the speaker, I consider opening the jewelry box. Only, it's not really my place to do it, so I wait.

I hear Pops approach with his familiar boot-dragging walk. I lean back, crossing my ankle over my knee, relaxed, nonchalant, pretending I'm negotiating from a position of power.

I like to think I'm a big guy, but Pops has an ominous presence. A wealthy cowboy. Tall, proud, and brutal.

Seeming irritated to have his internet bridge game interrupted, Pops sits in his leather chair and glowers, shifting his focus between Nonna and me.

I watch him the way a hunter would analyze the patterns and behaviors of his targets as Nonna starts in, explaining everything to Pops. It sounds trite when she tells it. Christa and I have fallen in love over the last month. We're ready to make a life together. Did it sound like that when I said it to her? So fast? The more she talks, I realize how Pops is going to say I'm being rash. Maybe even irresponsible.

"Isn't it romantic?" Nonna asks.

The fact that Pops is frozen-rope-focused on me should have

me concentrating on figuring out what I've done wrong lately, maybe apologizing for the spectacle I made by leaving the vet appointment earlier this afternoon. I guess it shows that I lack self-discipline just like he says. Even now, instead of worrying about Pops, it's Christa who returns, reigning my thoughts. As soon as I leave here, I'm going to find her.

"I'm familiar with your tactics." Pops's voice is stern and cold, making me match his icy stare.

"What do you mean by that?" I ask through gritted teeth.

His nostrils flare. "You're still on probation, living under our roof. You can't even manage to follow through on going back to school. Leland doesn't need you leading his daughter on or manipulating her into giving you a hand up you're not willing to work for yourself."

*He is absolutely full of shit.* I try to keep my temper and force myself to take a breath before responding. "I've done nothing but work my ass off to get back to where I was before I went to jail, but you'll never let me live it down. No matter what I do. I'm not manipulating Christa. I love her."

Pops's mouth presses into a firm slash. He makes a point of staring me down—a show of dominance. "Have you bothered to ask Leland what he thinks of your plan to marry his daughter?"

I'd intended to after I had the ring, and I stare right back at Pops, unwilling to be the first to look away.

Nonna frowns at him and checks to see how I'm managing. I'm not. Every bit the proud man my father raised, I'm furious. Does Pops genuinely think he has a say in this?

In a single, violent motion, he stands and swipes his hand through the air, cutting me off. "Let's get something clear. I will not tolerate you making a mockery of this family. You are to stop acting like a child."

*I hate you.* That's what I want to say, but instead, I stand and face him, stepping close and giving him a patronizing grin because I know it annoys him. "You just can't stand the idea that I might be happy without your permission."

"Once you've got your shit together, are off probation, living on your own, and have proved you've got your head out of your ass for a few years, you can think about getting married. In the meantime, you'll let Christa Blackburn move on with her life."

"I'm finished letting you tell me how to live, and I sure as hell won't let you tell me who to love." I turn to leave.

"You'll be walking away from West Creek."

"Are you threatening me?" I want to hear him confirm that after all the years I've cowered, it's come down to this.

He shrugs like it's self-evident. The answer has been in front of me all along.

I turn and walk away. This is it. I'm done being the spurned son.

Maybe marrying Christa will put me further out of favor with Pops. On the other hand, maybe I never had any hope of pleasing him, regardless. I was a fool to think I could impress him. So, instead of playing the part and capitulating like he wants me to, I bowed up, getting angry, truly furious, for the first time in months.

I let my temper flare until the heat inside me can't be contained.

"Charles," Nonna says from down the hall, "how could you?"

"Maybe we'll discuss the farm foreman job after the program meeting next Thursday," Pops says, like dangling the job I've dreamed of is going to stop me.

I'm already gone. I don't want to hear him lecture. *Keep your stupid rings, keep your opinions, and keep West Creek, because I quit.*

I'm so fucking done. I load my dogs in the truck and head out. It's ironic that I'm going for a nighttime drive to cool off after an argument with Pops the same way Dad did the night he died.

Without really thinking about it, I end up at my pheasant blind. It's late enough to be dark, but there's a full moon, which makes the place amazingly bright and clear. I pull on a sweatshirt to guard against the cool air and let the dogs roam the property. I do the same, entering the barn, climbing the ladder into the hayloft, and staring at the blanket I left there when I'd planned on romancing Christa.

It didn't work out exactly as I'd intended, but I wouldn't change it.

Can I plan the life I want to build with her and force it into existence, or will it become some other version I can't yet picture? A better version. That gives me hope. Starting with what we can afford now and considering ways to make more, enough to provide her with the kind of life she deserves. It's going to be hard, but being with her has made me whole. No way in hell am I letting Pops take that away from me.

But what if Leland disapproves? Maybe I should have asked, and shit if I have an answer for that, but I won't go back and live under Pops's control.

My mind moves too fast, identifying pitfalls and causing fear to pool inside me until I'm so agitated I need to move. Maybe it's the cool air that has me shaking. I can tell myself whatever I want. The trouble is I seldom believe my bullshit. Walking away from the ranch is going to be hard, near impossible to do forever, but I refuse to linger on what it might feel like right now, because someday the old man is going to keel over. Once he's gone, one way or another, I'll end up with what's mine.

Deep inside, I know whatever happens, I'm made with the same grit as the men who built the Corbett legacy. I'm going to make it through alright. So why wait? The time I spent in jail, the days I've spent working to earn Pops's trust, all of it has prepared me to go out on my own and prove myself. Every challenging circumstance that ever arrived in my life will help me win.

Then again, things aren't as bleak as they might have been

with Abner buying the tannery. Maybe we'll convince Leland to buy some land. One thing I know how to do is run a ranch. It won't make us rich right away, but it will be an honorable living, one where my efforts are appreciated.

Feeling energized, I whistle for the dogs, then load them in the truck and drive toward the tannery in hopes of finding Christa there and picking up where we left off last night.

I'm five minutes from town when my phone alerts with the blaring tone I've set up for a fire department call. I check the text and read:

> FIRE AT B&L FUR DRESSING REQUESTING ASSISTANCE FROM FIRE DEPARTMENTS IN TOWNS OF HIGGINS, WESLEY, WINDRIVER, MILFORD, PLT CTY HAZ MAT, GFD, WYOMING STATE PATROL, WGC AND WREA UTILTIES

My lungs startle and then seize.

I've never seen such a long list of first responders sent to a call.

I dial Christa's phone. It goes straight to voicemail.

I should go to the station, but instead, I press the throttle. The diesel engine roars as I push the speed up to a hundred miles an hour down the narrow country road. My thoughts are frantic, jumping from one thought to the next. Why won't she answer her phone?

It could be nothing—a small fire. But being inside the place, I'm aware of the chemical vats and tanning drums, the piles of dried furs and decades of hide dust. A simple fire could turn into an inferno.

Within a mile of town, I have to slow to avoid killing someone. Smoke carries on the cool summer air. An orange glow comes from the direction of the tannery.

Not good.

Around the last corner flames glow ominously. Only at

certain angles can I see walls. Three fire trucks are lined up along the street.

"Fucking hell, Christa, where are you? Please be safe." Mindful of my dogs in the back, I screech to a stop a distance away and leap from the truck to race toward the fire. The doors and windows are gone. Flames lick from the openings.

What if she's inside?

Even as part of me wants to find out, running in unprepared would be the worst possible choice. If I want a chance in hell at helping her, I need to stay composed.

I reach the fire trucks, locate Pete, my captain, and ask, "Is there a briefing?"

"Call came in from the neighbors about ten minutes ago. There were two explosions. A smaller one followed by a bigger one a few minutes later. It took the roof off. So far, we've been focusing on keeping the fire from spreading to neighboring structures."

Of course, whatever the co-op stores in their adjacent warehouses could be highly problematic, and a few residential structures will have to evacuate.

I almost can't manage to ask the question, but I force air into my lungs because I have no choice. "Anyone inside?"

"We don't know," he says, grim faced. "We just got here."

I know what I need to do. Get my gear. I'm going to need it. Focusing on my training is my only hope. I gear up as quickly as possible while trying to prepare myself mentally.

We don't see a lot of fires in town. The tannery is my first industrial fire.

And Christa could be inside.

I want to scream out her name and be rewarded by her running toward me. I can't stand the idea she might be trapped in that terror.

I suck in so much air I can't move. Can't inhale. All I can think of is smoke suffocation and burns.

Goddammit. I've never faced a moment like this or been so close to losing someone I love and felt so powerless to change it.

I know she usually parks around the rear near the loading dock, so as soon as I have my equipment on, I skirt the block, avoiding the worst of the damage to come through the alley. Fortunately, her truck isn't in its regular spot. My heart stutters back to life, but as I stare into the burning building that flicker of relief falters.

I wish she would answer her phone. I want confirmation that she's safe.

I turn full circle.

That's when I see her truck over at the co-op, but she's nowhere in sight.

She's got to be inside the tannery.

"Christa," I scream and race toward the lethal blaze—heat, noise, and pressure that no one could withstand for long. Even in flame-retardant gear, cold fear settles into my limbs, but I have training and a crew of firefighters on my side. I call Pete, "I'm pretty sure Christa is still inside. We need to send in a team."

"We can't do that," he says. "You know the rules."

Very strict procedures exist about when and when not to try for a fire rescue. Several apply to this situation, but I can't think about that now. If you cannot rescue the occupants without putting yourself in a position where the potential for death is high, do not attempt the rescue. This is an intense chemical fire in a building with a full basement. Chances are the floor is about to give way, if it hasn't already.

But I have to save her. *I don't have a choice.* I want to explain to him, but I don't have time.

My feet are moving forward. I'm making a plan, considering how I'm going in, where Christa might be, thinking perhaps she's near the back, trying to get to her truck.

"Carter," Pete's voice rings out from the speaker. "Do not go in there. Do you hear me?"

I enter the burned area through the southeast corner and

move forward by inches, independent of my better judgment, praying I'll find her safe amid the flames.

In what was once the office, fire comes from around and above, but the room itself is intact, giving me hope that she may still be safe somewhere inside. Knowing it's a risk, I push the dividing door to the tannery's main room and expose an abyss so hot and loud I can hardly think amid sparks and smoke. Burning debris drops into the room from above with regularity that's both terrifying and destructive.

*At least it's not coming from under the floor.* I take a step forward and test my footing. *I'm on a stable surface.*

The tannery floor, where the vaults were is a wreck, like something out of an action movie. A form moves in the distance ahead of me. *Christa.*

Hope makes me reckless. I take a huge step forward, over something engulfed in flames, placing my foot into an area I can't see. I stumble forward and catch myself an instant before I fall through a hole in the floor.

I push myself up and face my captain, soot covering his fire suit, anger written all over his face. I read his lips. "Told you not to come in here."

He grabs my arm as if intending to drag me back the way he's come.

I shake my head. "Christa. Have you seen her? Please, help me find her."

Flames cast an orange glow over his features, no longer angry but set in a hard mask. "We have to get out of here."

I pull away.

"I'm going." "I'll help you." We both speak at the same time.

We turn toward the inferno behind us and walk into the fire.

The radio on the captain's shoulder comes to life with a message. "We have her outside. Christa Blackburn is outside."

"Thank God," the captain says.

I don't realize I've been holding my breath until it bursts out of me on a whooshing exhale.

We take measured steps, retracing Pete's route to what used to be the front entrance.

They didn't say, *We have her safe outside.* Is she okay, unharmed? I can't breathe right, until I see her standing by the command post poking her finger toward the fire. "I need to go back in," she shouts.

The firefighter, a guy from our squad whose known each of us for a while, releases her then gives me a look. *He's afraid of her.*

It would be funny in other circumstances, but at least she's energetic enough to stand her ground and know what she wants.

I lift my helmet shield then grip her by the shoulders and look into her eyes, dark and wild with pain. "You can't."

"But I didn't get all the orders out."

She could have died in there, and I'm so furious at her for risking her life to get things out that I come unhinged and scream, "You could have died!"

"But I didn't. I got out." Her tone is soft, pleading even.

I pull my helmet off and stare at it. Her courage makes me even more determined to prove that I am worthy of this woman who is capable of knowing her limits and saving herself. Leland may not approve of me marrying her, and I need to prove that I deserve her.

I want to hold her to me, crush her fragile form and never let her get away, but then reality sinks in. My deal with Abner, everything I put on the line to buy her a chance, is burning to the ground. But I'm unwilling to talk about the deal I made with Abner, my intention to leave the ranch or any of it.

All I can think is what I scream in her face so loud and angry it's like someone else is shouting. "I needed you to trust me!"

"I do." She wraps her arms around me, and it's desperate and sad. The most painful hug, holding on for dear life as she sobs, leaving a wet spot on my overcoat. "I didn't mean for this to happen."

Christa releases her hold and gazes up at me. I feel dead inside, hopeless.

But it's not her that's making me furious. It's this deep, lingering doubt that Pops and Leland are right. Her life has just burned to the ground, and all I can think is she has no idea how difficult things have just become for me.

I pull her to me, whispering into her hair. "I'm so glad you're safe."

She looks up at me, and I add, "Darlin', I'm sorry for getting upset, and I know you want to do everything to save the orders, and I love that about you, but you can't go back in there."

Her arms tighten around me, then relax, and the truth of our mutual bond is in the way she's trusting me now; even when I'm not the man I need to be, she's teaching me who that man is, so I know what I need to do next.

# CHAPTER 23

## CHRISTA

Mix fertilizer drums, lingering odors, and faulty wiring with combustible dust and it turns into a roaring blaze.

Who knew? I should have taken the risks more seriously, but I grew up in the tannery. This is how Dad did things. I still can't fully believe it's happening. Shocked by the fierce energy of fire, and shaken to the core, I head home. I need to make sure Dad knows what happened and don't have a working phone, so it makes sense to go there in person.

When I park beside Dad's truck, I'm shaking and barely able to unbuckle my seatbelt or manage the old truck's stubborn door handle. This is bad. So bad.

Do they already know? Or am I going to have to tell them?

I push the front door open, and the familiar action feels different. Nothing in my life will ever be the same. It's the same old door, but the tannery is gone. This is a new, terrible reality.

Dad is at the kitchen table in his wheelchair. He sees me, and with that simple look, I don't know if he knows or not, but I start blubbering, gushing. I'm not sure how much of it makes sense, but Dad's rubbing his eyes when he says, "We're in escrow. We just got the deposit."

"No one looked at our books," I say, startled into focus. "Who's the buyer?"

"Some investor type. He talks through lawyers." Dad smiles, but it's a sad, heartbreaking smile. "Apparently our place with the permits and established reputation is as rare as a unicorn."

"They're paying us the asking price," Mom says. Her eyes gleam with genuine, sober excitement.

Dad says, "We should go save what we can."

There's nothing to save, but I can't say that. I can't even think. I'm too shaken to drive, so Mom takes the keys. Sober or not, she's managing to keep herself together better than I am right now. I'm lightheaded enough a sneeze would knock me over. *What have I done?*

As soon as we get close, the extent of damage is clear to all of us. Glistening tears streak down Dad's cheeks. Zombie-like, I follow my parents around the scene, learning details from the captain in charge. The co-op, a body shop, two nearby homes, and an apartment building have been evacuated. Residents crowd the street.

It takes forty firefighters from nine different departments to contain the blaze. Their efforts to save equipment and hides are heroic.

I burned the tannery to the ground. There's no one to blame but me. That's all I think. Over and over on repeat.

I know right where I went wrong, trying to multi-task without comprehending the risks, but that's a boring, worn-out story. There's no good explanation and any excuse sounds like poor me, why me, whining.

I'm still counting on the insurance, but I hate to bring it up to Dad. I need to get into his email, read the offer, figure out who the buyer is, and attempt to hold the deal together while filing an insurance claim, but I can't even focus on that because I'm too busy watching Carter. At first, he made trips into the undamaged part of the building, salvaging what he could before helping to make sure the structure comes down safely.

I can't peel my gaze away from him.

And that right there is the very root of my problem.

I long for him even as my infatuation has distracted me to the point I've ruined everything.

With a bulldozer, they demolish the remaining walls and clear the interior to get at pockets of fire, hot spots remaining under the hides.

If he notices me, he doesn't show it. He never looks at me. Not once.

I wait for him to take a break, but he doesn't.

My parents find me, saying they're ready to head home for the night. What's the point of staying when there's nothing we're allowed to do?

I doubt any of us will sleep. I need my email so I can find answers and make progress, so I go along with them, pressing my fingers to the glass as Carter passes out of sight.

As soon as we return to my parents' house, I get on the computer in Dad's study to find out more about the buyer. Like Dad said, the contract has come through a law firm that represents an LLC. There are no individual names on anything besides an attorney acting on their behalf. The buyer is intentionally anonymous, and I want to know why.

But I dig into the LLC's state regulatory filings and obtain the same information. An attorney representing a client.

Shifting gears, I read the insurance policy to learn what we'll need to file a claim.

Looking through the company's emails, I realize with a falling heart that a cancellation notice came last week.

I read it and reread it, but the meaning is still the same.

Our policy was canceled three weeks ago for non-payment.

Who was supposed to pay it? *Me.*

What was I doing when I should have been paying the bill? *Of course, I was falling in love with Carter.*

I came home, promising Dad I could help him turn the tannery around, and I burned it to the ground.

I've done more damage by coming home than I've helped. My head is too heavy to hold up. I rest my forehead on the bills strewn across the desk.

The shame is more than I can bear. It condemns me even as I feel a responsibility and a strong desire to hide this latest disaster long enough that I can fix it.

Only, I have no way of fixing anything. A ragged sob escapes, breaking over me with such force I can't stop the flood of tears.

"Christa." It's Dad's voice. "Stop crying."

I lift my head only long enough to speak. It's pathetic, I know, but I'm beaten and broken and so frickin' tired. "I can't help it," I say to Dad. "I'm so sorry."

He moves in as close as his wheelchair will allow and puts a comforting hand on my back. He rubs back and forth, soothing me like I'm a baby all over again. Like I'm still his little girl. A hard sob racks me.

"I ruined *everything.*"

"You've got to stop trying to fix everything," he says.

*Stop trying?* That tired instruction combined with Dad's patient love energizes my weary mind.

"I can't stop. Not ever." *I let this happen. It's all my fault.* "I will fix it." *If it takes my last breath. I will die trying.*

A sad smile tugs at his lips. "I was tired of having the tannery."

He's infuriating when he lies like this. I won't let him get away with it. "You had it sold."

"Maybe," he says. "Maybe not. Either way, I'm glad it's over."

He's not making any sense now and I'm ready to prove it. "How can you be glad?"

"I just am."

I lay the worst of it on the line, expecting he'll finally see things from my side. Still, I try to soften the blow. "Our insurance lapsed."

"Well . . ." This latest news takes him back, but he recovers faster than a marathoner after a sprint. Offering me a small smile, he says, "I guess you can't try to improve it anymore."

"That's not fair. I was trying to keep it going for you and Mom."

"Christa." Just the one word spoken in his baritone lets me know our conversation is shifting. He's not angry but he's done coddling me. "You're using us as an excuse."

I hold up my hands in mock surrender and ask, "Why would I do that?"

He takes a breath then lets it out slowly, making me wait an ungodly long time for his response. "Because you think our happiness is more valuable than your own."

*It is more valuable.* But I don't say that, because I can't stand to tell him that after he sacrificed so much to help me get into college, I lied about why I came home.

"Sweetheart," Dad says. "You have to take care of yourself."

"I didn't know how to survive on my own. That's why I came home."

"I know," he says, knocking the wind right out of me. "And you didn't have to lie. You don't have to be ashamed of growing up and struggling and not knowing what to do. Sometimes you're going to make mistakes. All I expect you to do is learn from them."

"I have learned."

He raises one eyebrow so high it's almost cartoonish.

No matter how much I love his silly looks, I'm not taking the bait. I refuse to smile, and instead ask, "Why can't you see that I have to fix this?"

"Some things can't be fixed. There are times when you can only move on."

"No. No, Dad. I can't leave this and . . ." Then I'm sobbing again. He holds me for I'm not sure how long, but I cry so much.

Dad holds me until there are no more tears to cry. "I love you, Ducky. Mom loves you. We don't expect you to step in and rescue us. We want you to live."

Dad's use of my childhood nickname takes me back to all the times he supported me growing up. Whatever I came up with—usually involving water, first a slip-n-slide in the yard, then swimming, then rowing—he was there to help me. Always so strong and capable. "But you're sick. You need me now."

"I do need you," Dad says. "But not the way you think."

"Then tell me what to do."

His eyebrows draw together. "Haven't I tried?"

"Then try again, please. I'm listening now."

Dad moves away. The separation between us feels symbolic of the conversation turning a corner. "Date. Have fun. Live. Stop worrying about our finances. Stop trying to come to my appointments."

"But—"

"No but. See, this is my fault. I was going to fire you, but you were seeing Carter. Maybe I should have gone ahead with it, but I decided to wait and fire you if you broke things off with him."

"Fire me?"

"You refuse to listen. It was going to take something drastic to get through to you."

"That's not fair."

"You're a little like your mom," he says, with a chuckle.

"No," I reply because *no*. "She's a drama queen."

"You're dramatic in your own way."

I give him my version of the cartoon eyebrow.

He gives me a half-smile, then says, "You rushed in to fix everything. You need to learn that you can't control my choices, just like your mom can't control my choices, just like you can't control her choices. See what I'm saying?"

I see what he's saying and I'm curious, so I ask, "Let's say you fired me. What happens to you?"

"I try to sell the tannery. If I don't, I let the old-timers work when they want. They pay me a little for whatever they make to cover the utilities and taxes. Otherwise, it sits."

"What about money?"

He shrugs.

Unwilling to accept his silence, I ask, "How would you afford to live?"

"I've requested a payout from an annuity we put in years ago. It would be tight for a while, but my disability claim is almost through. I'll get social security in a few years."

"So . . ."

"So, it's not your problem."

"Okay," I reply, feeling a weight shift inside me.

Dad folds his hands in his lap, a gesture that means our debate has escalated. He's about to bring out the big guns. "What if I told you I want to use the annuity to repay your loans?"

"You can't. I won't let you."

He offers me a little smile. "Hasn't it always been your dream to get away from Higgins?"

"It was." Until I fell in love with Carter. Now, I'm not so sure.

"Then I'm glad the tannery's gone. I don't have to fight with you to convince you to focus on what's important to you."

It's easy for him to say this now. He wants to make me feel better, but his life's work just went up in flames. There's no insurance payout on the way. He just lost on the sale. "You can't really mean that you're glad."

"It's just money," he says.

"You could buy me a decent house," Mom says from the other room. "And some new furniture. We could take a vacation."

"See?" Dad says. "I've got everything I need right here."

"We *need* a new refrigerator," Mom says as she walks toward him to drive her point home.

"I'm surrounded by the people I love," Dad replies and tugs her into his lap.

Mom glares at me for so long that I give voice to the animosity between us. "Whatever's on your mind, just say it."

Tilting her head down, she gives me an introspective frown, then says, "You could have died in there, Christa. Do you have any idea what that would have done to me?"

I realize both of my parents love me more than any figure in their bank account, and the knowledge slides around me like a warm embrace. I've done so much damage trying to convince myself I can hide from what's behind me, cemented into the past.

"I have a problem," I confess, opening up to my parents for the first time in years. "I have a hard time taking responsibility for my mistakes. I get freaked out. I lose focus on everything else. I can't even function straight."

They're on the same page for once and sit staring at me, seeming sure I have more to say.

"You want me to move on with my life and date, but I can't handle having a life outside of surviving day to day; trying that cost me my college scholarship. Being with Carter cost you the tannery."

Dad sits up in his wheelchair. "Let's get something straight. No one knows what started that fire. The wiring is old. The equipment is old. It's not like anything's been maintained the way it should have been. You didn't do anything to deserve blame for this."

Mom leans in and cocks her head, a gesture that has me on edge. "Tell me you don't believe you're responsible for everything wrong with that place. I raised you better than to believe that nonsense."

"When we fell in love," Dad says, looking at Mom with

hearts in his eyes, "I promised you the world. We had so many plans."

"Most of them never happened," Mom says.

Dad squeezes her to him, and she smiles. "I'm not saying I'd change it."

Watching them, I hear Dad's words about how they were raised and recall what Carter said about my parents. Some marriages will always be like theirs. It's not my place to decide whether their marriage is broken or wrong. It's theirs, and seeing Mom, sitting on Dad's lap, I think they're going to be okay.

Maybe there is no perfect love story. There's only love.

Precious, powerful, and terrifying.

# CHAPTER 24

CARTER

*The Higgins Tribune* publishes an article, including an interview with Leland about the tragedy. The reporter says the investigation is ongoing and may take weeks because hot spots remain under the hides. Nobody knows how long first responders will have to monitor the area. It's a spectacle no one in town has seen before. People rally around Christa's family with well-wishes and offers to help.

After making a questionable deal with Abner in exchange for his purchase of the tannery, I tried and failed to get him to follow through; how, indeed, could I force him to buy something that had burned to the ground? He owes me now, and maybe things are better that way.

My back and neck are tense with worry and exhaustion as I plan ahead, leaning into what's coming next for us because that's the only option I have. Only it's all sideways of what I'd hoped.

If anyone would have asked me how my life was going to turn out, I never would have imagined West Creek would end up being a place I no longer belong. But it seems that's what it will take to help me become my own man.

I've dealt with my feelings about Pops and faced the facts. I've been stuck in the past for too long, burdened by blame and anger.

Walking away will be near impossible, made worse because in this rural part of the state—primarily agricultural, with the majority of its land owned by ranchers who have worked the same place their entire lives—relationships are highly concentrated, both in their sense of community and in their loyalty to principle. The opinions of those who have lived for generations on a piece of land carry weight, and any decision made or action taken by one family tends to be carried by others. Meaning that my choice to leave the ranch on poor terms is taken seriously not just by Pops but by every rancher in the vicinity, who must weigh any decision to hire me both strategically and personally.

Behind the scenes, flurries of phone calls carry gossip and opinions, but I tell myself they mean no harm.

When Jackson Becker, a local rancher who runs a small operation near the county line, tells me he will need to talk to Pops before he can make a hiring decision, I tell him that I understand. It's just the way things are in areas of the world with small populations consisting of generational families.

It doesn't surprise me when Jackson turns me down the following day. I have a criminal past, and seriously, who would want to get on the wrong side of Pops? *No one.*

While I could coerce Max into giving me half the money the grandparents gave him and live off it for a while, I want to prove something, not just to Pops, but also to myself.

It takes less than a day to find a temporary job up by Laramie as a hand for a guy I met through Jake's dad, Colt. I don't make a show of leaving, but load up my dogs, pack what I need, and stop at Christa's on my way out of town.

I thought leaving West Creek would be hard, but facing her is the hardest part.

I won't tell her what Pops said about marrying her or that I'm leaving because of our argument. So instead, as she stands just outside her front door, I say, "I'm sorry, darlin'. I don't want to go, but I can't stay in a town where I can't work."

"You're leaving?" Her voice cracks. Even though this is one of the best possible scenarios, her quiet words threaten to wreck me. I would stay if she asked me to.

"We'll keep in touch." When she looks down, I press my palms to her cheeks and tilt her face up to make her hear me. "I'll call you every night." I pull her into me and smell her hair and whisper, "I love you." But I don't expect that she'll wait for me. Why would she want to?

She steps forward. Close enough that her body presses to mine.

Maybe it's the fact we've both lost everything. Or maybe it's the pain in her expression that makes me take a step toward her. She backs up one step, then another. I don't want to go. She doesn't want me to go. We both know it's for the best, but our feet keep moving.

Without a word, she's drawn me inside, past the living room and into her bedroom, where she closes the door. We stand, looking at each other. Her cheeks are hollow as she draws in a breath. I'll never forget the look in her eyes or the emotion in her voice when she tells me, "I want you."

Then everything inside me needs her. I can't not be with her. I fist the back of my collared shirt and jerk it over my head. Word-lessly, Christa peels her tank top off and pulls me tight against her, skin to skin. All I can think is I've wasted so much life not having Christa.

Kissing her hard and hot, I back her into the closed door. I taste her mouth and want to taste all of her, a frustrated groan emerges from deep inside me.

Raw desire drives me toward her.

She shifts, pulling me with her as she backs toward the bed.

I wrap my arms around her, lift her off her feet, swinging her onto the mattress. She looks at me sideways with a slow smile then comes up on her knees, moving toward me in her jeans and bra.

Christa is tempting beyond words, and the vulnerable way she's waiting for me to make the next move drives the worries out of my mind, making me crush her to my chest, never wanting to let her go.

Then her fingers tease my waistband, making my cock twitch for her hand. Then she's feeling me through my jeans, arousing me even more. I grit out, "Sweet Jesus."

She scoots forward, grinding against me until all I can think is I will never be able to let her go, and this is wrong. The thought of her suffering or shedding a single tear over me is enough to make me pull back.

"Darlin', we can't."

"I just want to touch you," she whispers against my neck.

I'm wondering how long I'll be able to endure this torture without dying, knowing that she will now take me in her sweet hand. She opens my fly to free me, then strokes me, palming me, finding a slow-burning rhythm that makes me want to bury myself deep inside her. I can't though, not when I'm on my way out of town with nothing to offer her.

Attempting to distract myself, I grip her breast, not wanting to release her mouth but wanting to taste her skin while pulling her tight against me. It's all too much. Too long waiting. Too many nights spent wondering—too much pleasure.

She grips me tightly, roughly enough to make me stop reaching for her. She shifts her weight and strains away to unfasten her belt, sliding her jeans and panties down her hips.

I want a moment to see her, to touch her and learn about her, but her hands go to my shoulders, mine find her ass, then she says, "Lay on your back." And how can I say no? Then she's over me, moving down, and I move up, and we are suddenly very close.

So many emotions flood me: panic, elation, irritation, desire.

My breath hitches as she strokes my erection, taking it in one hand and guiding me to her entrance and welcoming me inside her hot, slickness. Desire draws my balls up, sending buzzing tension up my spine. "Condom, darlin'. We can't."

I barely breathe as she begins to move. She understands what she's doing when she begins sliding over me until I'm fully inside, skin to skin. I close my eyes and try to think, but she moans. Then she shows me she knows what she's doing, riding me like getting me off is her sole focus in the world until I'm on the verge of doing the unthinkable. I've never in my life been inside a woman bare, let alone had the pleasure of—"Oh my holy God." I'm half lifting her, half hoping to fail to separate us, to get out of her because as much as I want to have that son we have talked about, we're not ready for this. But she's working on me, her rhythm matching my thrusts, moaning the sexiest sound.

My vision is blurring over. I close my eyes. "You have to slow down." I pull her hips until she's seated on me. She moans then starts to move again, slow at first then faster. I feel her body tensing, finding what she needs. My hands follow her hips, holding her, wanting her, claiming her.

Her body clenches around me as she moans, "Yes, yes, yes, please, Carter," causing me to lose my mind. I groan as she moves, sinking into her even deeper. She's kissing me when I start to come, making no attempt to pull out. She collapses on top of me, and I hold her, stroking her hair as our breathing returns to normal. We both know what we just did.

She brings her mouth to mine, staying close even after we're no longer kissing.

I flip her over, trying to see her face and read her emotions and regain some sense of control over myself and the situation. Framing her with my arms, holding myself above her mostly naked body with my hips wedged between her thighs, I place soft kisses on her lips and whisper, "I've loved you for years."

When she doesn't say it back, conflicting emotions crush against each other inside me until it's almost too much to contain. Her silence is my answer.

I gaze at this woman below me, who is strong and trying not to cry.

Christa has given me everything. I can't catch a breath or complete a rational thought. I know she's trying to put up a wall.

We did what we did.

"Darlin'." I'm unsure what words I will say next.

She turns her face away and blinks hard. "You should go."

It's like I've been gut punched. Christa wants me to go.

Maybe she doesn't want me the way I want her.

Pops's words reverberate through my tense body. *Leland doesn't need you leading his daughter on or manipulating her into giving you a hand up you're not willing to work for yourself.*

Now's my time to leave before I say something I regret. *You're the center of my world. Please come with me. Please wait for me.* So much pressure weighs on her already. My leaving will make things easier for her, allowing her to figure out what she truly wants. I'm not the best option for a smart girl like her. I have nothing without the promise of a ranch that doesn't belong to me.

I move in a daze, yanking on my shirt, fastening my jeans, and walking out the door, white-knuckling the gear shift as I put the truck in drive, catching a final glimpse of her standing outside in the rearview mirror. My heart shatters.

I promised her things that weren't mine to give. I screamed at her about trust when I haven't trusted her with my secrets. I haven't told her the truth about Max, about Abner, about much of anything. I should have told her about the deal I was making with Abner, but would she have tried to stop me the way I wanted to stop her from working so hard at the tannery and taking so many risks?

Fact is, I owe her an apology. Plain and simple. Then I owe her the truth.

Maybe I'm still too selfish to let her go, and that's why I did what I just did when I know it was wrong, but part of me hopes leaving will prove I'm worth more than Pops says. That away from here, I'll find a new way forward that allows me to set things right with Christa.

# CHAPTER 25

## CHRISTA

I'VE BEEN TELLING myself men are a distraction, and I'm convinced it's true because I woke up this morning feeling Carter's arms wrapped around me. His lips near my ear. His breath tickling the hairs at my neck. I shift and roll over to tell him I love him, but I wake up alone and press my face into the pillow, hoping my overactive brain will let me go back to sleep.

It's a nice dream. It would be fabulous if I could live life as I see it when I'm asleep. But, instead, as the date I'm supposed to start my cycle nears, I spring to my feet, propelled into action by worry about our one reckless moment. I'm really not like that girl who wanted him so badly she claimed him while he was trying to leave, or so I tell myself as I reiterate for the zillionth time that I'm not even late yet. But I am that girl, aren't I? I could have gotten a morning-after pill, but I didn't. Still, I can barely breathe from the pressure of fear closing in on me. I stare at my exhausted face in the bathroom mirror thinking there's no way I could a handle an infant, and yet, it would be my luck to turn up pregnant with Carter working in Laramie.

As good as it was to be with him, neither of us was thinking clearly.

A profound sense of loss accompanies that thought. After a month of telling myself I was only having fun, I'm still trying to put my heart back together.

Because I'm still clinging to the most savage emotion known to mankind—hope. Hope that Carter will show up at my door unannounced. Hope that we can make this last despite the distance. Hope that I wasn't a complete fool to fall in love.

Evidence for my heart's case, super-gluing it together, is how we talk on the phone every night. He asks me to tell him jokes. At first, I had a hard time coming up with something funny to say when my entire being felt so destroyed, but now I enjoy finding something more outlandish each day than the day before, because he's sad too, and both of us need to smile.

Still, I feel us drifting. How long will he be happy listening to me tell him stupid jokes?

The thing is, I understand why he left. He was living under an incredible amount of pressure from his grandparents. I've come up with many scenarios, but instead of trying to decipher the past, which has led me into spiraling sadness for weeks, I tell myself it's for the best that he's gone.

An opportunity to focus is what I wanted.

My entire body rebels against that idea, making me miserable in an attempt to course correct and aim me toward a future where Carter and I are together.

Still in my pajamas, I drag myself from the bathroom to the desk I put where the couch used to be. I turn my attention to setting up an accounting system for one of my new clients, while attempting to pump myself up about the job at hand—what having my own business means for my future. Applying what I learned in school within the tiny town of Higgins, I founded an administrative support and bookkeeping service vibrant enough to keep me busy sixty hours a week with setups and software integrations. Skyler was my first customer, letting me fix her up with a system to streamline her finances and provide instant information for her salon. Once word got out, I was bombarded by local entrepreneurs within days—mostly independent contractors with only one employee, a few smaller ranchers, and two of the Corbetts' homesteaders—who are thankful for someone to do their paperwork and thrilled to have accurate, up-to-date information about their finances.

It's easy and rewarding work that pays decently, and sticking to my plan could mean I'll have my student loans paid off before I die at eighty-three.

According to my spreadsheet, it's not actually that hopeless, and I'm working extra hard to save money on every little thing, so when Emily calls and invites me out for coffee, I ask for a rain check.

"Pay it forward," she says, referring to the day we met and invoking an offer I can't turn down even though I know she's gotten back together with Colt, and Colt and Carter have become fast friends. I dress haphazardly and meet her at the cafe.

"I don't want to talk about Carter," I say as soon as I sit across from her at the small table she's selected near a window.

"I know." She gives me a mom look.

I grin back at her. "I bet that look works better on Jake."

"It doesn't even work on him anymore." Emily fakes a sulk then smiles.

It's good to see her happy, partly due to Jake's progress in his fight against leukemia, which is going better than the doctors hoped. Maybe Jake is one of the lucky ones. We've all got our fingers crossed, and no one wants to jinx him by talking about it too much.

"Tell me about Colt." He's her favorite topic of late.

She talks fast about how good he's been with Jake. How great it feels to be a family again. How Carter helped to bring them together.

I give her a look.

"Sorry," she says. "I know you don't want me to talk about him."

"It's not that I don't want to."

"Then what is it?" I should have known she would bite on that.

No way she's letting me off easily, so I say, "Everyone keeps asking when he's coming back, and it's hard for me to admit even to myself that I don't know if he'll ever be back."

"Did you ask him?"

My melancholy mood turns into stony silence that edges toward a meltdown. I stare at the coffee shop's walls, tacked with years of flyers about all kinds of past events along with some that are still coming up.

Emily sips her coffee, waiting patiently, wearing me down without saying a word.

I sigh, my voice holds zero enthusiasm for talking about this. "I don't want to pressure him." Or have him tell me it's over.

"You have to talk to him."

"Yeah. I know."

"I'm going to say something, and you can tell me to shut it, but he talks to Colt about you."

I really shouldn't want to know what Carter says to his friend in confidence, but I can't help my own insecurity or the hope making my heart beat faster. "What does he say?"

"I get the impression it was hard for him to leave you, but he thought it was best for you. Something about not having anything to give you without the ranch."

After all the worry I've put into possibly being pregnant, I'm ready to rush to the store and buy a test. But instead, my period arrives that afternoon. I'm not pregnant.

Part of me—a silly, irresponsible part—feels hollowed out and sad by the loss of an imagined pregnancy, but also, I feel oddly free to consider what I would have done if I were pregnant. I wasn't willing to entertain such reckless thoughts while pregnancy seemed inevitable and life-altering.

Still, I would have told Carter. He would have come home and made peace with his grandparents. I would have hated to see him do it, but he would have done it for us. For me. For our baby. I know that like I know my truth. And it wrecks me to love him, and it will shatter me forever to lose him.

Trust doesn't come easily to me. It never has.

But as I read stupid jokes on internet sites and watch puppy videos that make me smile even when I'm sad, I think of how he was with his dogs. He was affectionate and silly while he was at the ranch, and he took them with him to Laramie even when many people would have left them behind for the hardship they created.

That might not mean much to some, but it shows he has a genuine heart. He's not in this for himself. Getting the ranch was always about his family, those he's lost and those he hopes to protect.

He chased me when I said no. He held me when I was hurting. Ever since we were in grade school, he's been special to me. I'm going to push aside my fear and chase him. Tonight.

I'm ready to take a leap of faith.

Truth is, I should've done it by now.

Instead of coming up with a joke, I scour ads for a cheap place in Laramie.

I load my truck with everything I'll need to live and keep up with my customers, and because I have to, I stop by my parents' house on the way out of town.

My hands shake when I grab the doorknob, and when I walk into the kitchen, I'm a little lightheaded about what I'm about to do. I pause to regain my sense of purpose. I'm leaving. I love them, but I'm leaving. I'll come to visit and call all the time. Nothing bad will come of my leaving home. This isn't like going to New York.

Dad's looking a little better today than he has the last few days, and it does my heart good to see him working on taxidermy. He loves it, and the mule deer rack in front of him is a beast with non-typical antlers, extra heavy and wide enough to set a record.

"Whose?" I ask, pointing at the deer.

"Andrew's," Dad says. "He brought this beast down with a bow."

"Hard to believe," I reply, even though it's not. There are colossal deer all over the place around here, and while I like goading Dad, I don't want to talk about Andrew even though he's likely to come up again when I tell Dad what I'm doing.

"What's going on with you?" Dad asks.

"Nothing," I say because I'm cowardly and reluctant to explain why I'm smiling for the first time in a while. "Why?"

"You look different. Happier. Is it Carter? Did he move back?"

"Geez, Dad, you know me." And he does. I grin while I try not to smile. Unfortunately, my face probably looks like a puzzle factory gone wrong. I'm waiting for him to say he doesn't approve.

"So . . ."

"I'm moving to Laramie."

I expect ridicule, even stunned silence, but Mom comes into the room and tugs on my hair, fixing it so the unruly lock is tucked behind my ear. "Our girl's finally come to her senses."

"Yeah," I say. I should have known she was eavesdropping from the other room, but I don't really care because she's been sober for a few days straight, which could be setting a new record—an event worth celebrating if I didn't worry mentioning it would send her into a relapse.

"What about Andrew?" I ask, feeling I've let Dad down.

Mom looks at Dad and laughs, and it's clear my parents think I'm hilarious.

"I mean it, Dad, are you disappointed in me?"

"I'm worried about you," he says, "but that doesn't mean I'm against your decisions. I'm glad to see you living what you think is best."

"I heard Andrew's dating Skyler, anyway," Mom says.

"You're kidding me." They've been friends forever, but Skyler hasn't been home enough to fill me in on her dating exploits and she's always sworn off dating Andrew.

Mom pops a shoulder. "Now that he won that Smithsonian prize for his Apache sculpture, he's going to take her out to Washington with him."

"You're kidding me," I repeat, not jealous but even more shocked.

"I'm not." Mom shakes her head in mock frustration. Her mouth is cocked to one side like she's about to lay it on thick, and she barely stops smiling as she pats me on the butt. "So go on, find that Corbett boy. Kiss him on the mouth."

Dad snorts.

Their laughter is contagious, and soon, both my parents are collapsed into themselves, shaking, trying not to snort out loud. Then, overtaken by hysteria, they lean back, giggling like children. Neither cares that I'm staring at them in stunned silence. Suddenly, it doesn't seem to matter because I'm laughing too.

I don't stay long. Once I'm in the truck, Mom makes me roll the window down so she can give me a bag of cookies for the road. She made them because they're supposed to relieve stress, which might help with Dad's MS (or so she says). I make her promise they don't contain anything that will make driving unsafe, then head east as the sun sets behind me.

The windows in my old truck rattle against the wind.

As I drive, I'm thankful for Dad and Mom. They could be the parents who tell me what not to do. I'm already afraid enough. If they'd added to my list of possible pitfalls, I would have fought with them, maybe even given in to their concerns.

I'm on the interstate, blasting a playlist I made one day while I was missing Carter. Of course, I included our song. I belt it out, singing my heart out as the truck races across the Wyoming countryside, telling myself I'm not insane to rent an apartment and move across the state in an afternoon.

When Carter calls at our usual time, I'm maybe forty minutes away from Laramie.

# CHAPTER 26

CARTER

Working at the first job available, I finally learn that life has been waiting for me to grab the reins. I left my safety net when I walked away from my family. Working on a ranch, without the pressure or politics of Pops's attitude, is rewarding in its own way, but there's no security living in a stranger's bunkhouse.

I enjoy the hard, back-breaking work, usually done by the lowest ranking hands, mending fences in the bitter wind, feeding cattle on the worst weather days, and staying up all night with pregnant heifers.

It doesn't matter what I have to do. I enjoy it because every step is one step closer to being a man Leland would respect. A man I respect.

But I miss Christa. Something fierce aches inside me at the thought of her suffering or shedding a single tear over me. I hope she doesn't cry. I hope she never cries over me.

Still sweaty from a hard day of grunt work as a low man on a ranch, worked primarily by older, more seasoned cowboys—who like to give me a hard time because they didn't come from massive family ranches like mine—I lay with my legs splayed forward. My back rests against the bumpy wall at the head of the bunk I've called home for the past month.

*Jail was worse,* I tell myself as I listen to the phone ring and wait for Christa to pick up.

When she answers, road noise comes across in the background, making my ears perk up like Job's do whenever I put on my shoes.

"Where are you?" I want to know everything about her, what she did today, where she went, and whether she had fun.

Maybe my senses are all hyper-aware about her, but I swear her breath hitches. She's about to lie. About what? I can't guess. My curiosity about her day turns into something slightly bitter and much less admirable. I decide not to push her.

"Tell me you're not speeding," I say, even though not knowing why she was going to lie kills me. It's better this way. Not making her life harder. She shouldn't feel pressured.

"I'm not speeding," she says, and something reassuring is in her voice. I'd bet my favorite trail saddle she's smiling. "I'm on the interstate, headed east. Well . . . but I think the road just turned south."

She's teasing me, and I'm unsure how to take it. Do I ask her again to tell me where she is? Or let it go? I go for full-bore cheesy. "At least your voice is still sexy."

Instead of taking the bait, she asks, "Want to hear a joke?"

"Is it guaranteed to make me laugh?" I ask because this is what we do, and as much as I miss her, I like that she's taking the time during the day to find a joke to tell me. I like it maybe too much.

"Knock, knock," she says.

"Who's there?"

"When where."

"When where who?"

"Tonight, Laramie, you and me."

*Holy shit.* I can't help the way I'm smiling as I spring up in bed. "Really?"

"Did you want to see me?" she asks, sounding smug.

Warmth blooms in my belly at the thought of her coming to see me. "Goddammit, woman, more than heaven itself."

"I like hearing that. Say it again."

Then she laughs.

Maybe it's the sweet tone of her happiness or the hot longing in my stomach, but I'm stunned. How is it she's come here? And why? To see me for the night? On a Tuesday?

Still, as soon as I compose myself, I hear myself say, "I'll get us a room and take you to dinner." Even as my heart pounds with yearning, excitement, and fear.

"You don't have to get us a room," she says.

A war rages inside me, and I try to hold my voice even. "Tell me what you want me to do."

"Come to my place, help me unpack?" she says nonchalantly.

My mind takes a few beats to catch up. Her place. Laramie. Unpack. "Fucking hell, Christa, you can't move here." *I wouldn't say I like it here.*

"Why?" she asks, speaking in her devastated voice. The one word breaks me.

"I didn't mean it like that. I want you with me *always*. I just . . . I sort of hate it here." *It would be best if you didn't see me like this.*

"You want me to turn around? Go home?"

"No, of course not."

"Then, what? I want to be with you. Do you want me with you?"

"Darlin', you have no idea how bad."

"I'm in love with you, and I'm not turning around. I'm half an hour away. Maybe twenty minutes now."

"And where's this place you've got to live?"

She gives me the address and says it's an apartment over

somebody's garage, and I have no idea what the hell she's thinking, but I love her so much I can barely talk as I hang up the phone after explaining that I've still got to shower if she wants me to smell half-decent when she sees me.

I race to get ready, and I'm grateful that I arrive ahead of her. It's nothing fancy, but from the outside, it looks clean, and the neighborhood is decent.

She pulls up, and her truck makes a noise I haven't noticed before.

I resolve here and now to learn about fixing trucks. I soak it all in as she pulls up and parks behind my truck. Then she's leaping out. Her voice, clothes, scent, and touch make me lose my mind. I'm still half-afraid this is a dream.

I crush her to me until she pulls away and puts her hands on her hips to study the apartment. "Pretty good for short notice."

"How short?" I ask.

"I started looking this afternoon while trying to find a joke for us."

"No shit." I step back and take her in. Fearless and real. So incredibly real and fantastic. "What'd your parents say?" I ask, sure of Leland's disapproving reaction.

She gives me a slight, satisfied shrug. "They were glad, happy to see me happy."

"No," I reply, figuring she's full of it. "You're trying to make me feel better about stealing you away."

"My mom said verbatim, 'You should've done it by now. Go kiss that boy on the mouth.'"

"You're serious?"

She nods.

I grin. "Kiss me."

"Okay," she whispers. She gazes at me for a long moment, then her eyes close, and our lips meet.

I remember her, taste her, and want her so bad I'm crazy to get closer. I suck her bottom lip into my mouth. My hands pull her toward me by the hips, holding her, wanting her, claiming her. "Sweet Jesus," I whisper. "This is the best surprise ever."

If we stand in the street kissing any longer, we will pass the point of arousal suitable for public display. With a commendable effort, I step back, ignoring her protesting moan. "Let's get your keys."

Later that night, we move all the things she brought out of her pickup into the one-room apartment. It's small and drafty. Nothing like I thought I'd give the woman I plan to marry, but she's given me an incredible gift by coming here, and I'm not about to pick it apart.

Even as I struggle to find my footing away from my family and all it's meant to be a Corbett, she's here by my side, making my life worth living.

We go on like that from one day to the next until she asks me if I wouldn't rather stay over with her than sleep at the bunkhouse. It's not a tricky question to answer.

After that, things start to get better for me all around. Not only is Christa a good influence on my otherwise gloomy moods, but she's also a wiz in business. She helps my boss put together a bookkeeping system to streamline his expenses. That opens a door for me to talk to him about the breeding plans and tracking system I'd been using at West Creek.

Little by little, we make progress, proving ourselves. It takes nine months for me to get promoted to farm manager of this small ranch in the eastern part of my home state, but every hour of work is worth it when I use the money I earned to buy Christa a ring.

I can see our life together play out, and it doesn't matter where we live or what we have as long as we have each other. We can handle what comes.

The velvet box is in my pocket, and my hands shake whenever I open it.

I'm going to ask her tonight. I want to do it right, and that's what's on my mind as I sit atop Ace, another man's horse, staring out at a hundred head of cattle that don't belong to my family or me but that I tend to with so much care they might as well be my children.

With a crackle of static, my radio comes alive at my hip. When I answer, Jim, the owner, says, "Your brother's here."

It's startling that he's here. I didn't see Max before I left, and I'm more than a little surprised he's driven to Laramie to see me when he could have called, but then again, I haven't returned his calls, not wanting to talk about coming back until I'd proved what I set out to prove.

I'm also a little pleased to see him.

I head for the barn to put up my horse and call Christa and let her know, asking if she wants to see him. There was a time I wouldn't have wanted her present for a visit like this with Max, but we've talked about everything at this point. I apologized for trying to set up Abner as a buyer for the tannery without letting her know what I was doing and for not trusting her to understand what I was trying to accomplish. In the end, she laughed it off. I could see it hurt that I'd kept things from her, but she seemed to admire my desire to ensure we ended up together.

I even told her about the history between Max and me.

Maybe it's all that history that makes her refuse to join us, saying it's better if Max and I deal with our brotherly shit without her opinions in the mix. Still, it's probably better she isn't there. Delaying more, I brush Ace down before seeing my little brother for the first time in almost a year.

Once I've put Ace away, I decide to keep Max waiting a little longer. Seeing him digs up all the reasons I haven't been talking to him since I left and excavates my regrets. I shower in the bunkhouse and change into clean clothes and boots. Making him wait is a prick move, but why is he here? Why now? Why not call?

When I finally see him in the driveway, he's leaning against his West Creek truck, which is still a match to mine.

He looks the same, smug and wearing his work clothes like he couldn't bother to put something else on before he drove three hours to see me.

A few minutes later, we're sitting in his pickup, rolling down the drive.

"Fucking Pops," he says, looking out the window with a furrow on his brow.

The sentiment hangs in the air as the truck rumbles down the main road leading into Laramie.

As much as I resent him for it, I wait for him to explain.

Wyoming dust billows in clouds behind us while an argument plays out in the muscles at Max's jaw.

Then he asks, "Remember when you convinced me to moon that bus of girls?"

Cracking a smile, I nod. "It turned out to be the swim team from Jackson."

"I never would have done it if you hadn't been goading me."

I focus on the dashboard, remembering how he'd had to hold himself up and pull his pants down, bracing himself while laughing hysterically. Shaking my head at the memory, I ask, "What made you think of that?"

"Just . . . the good times, you know?"

"Yeah," I say, even though I have a hard time remembering many good times between us since everything's gone to shit.

I tell him where to stop so we can eat, noting he still hasn't completed his thought about Pops. I'm not the only one remembering all the not-so-good times. Tires crunch gravel as he pulls into the parking lot of a diner not too far from where Christa and I live. I wonder if he knows that, but I don't voice the thought. *What would be the point?* I'm not going to invite him over or expect him to mail us a Christmas card. But I might invite him to the wedding if Christa wants me to. He is family, after all.

I meet him around the front of the truck. "What were you getting at about Pops?"

"Oh." Max takes a step toward me and puts his hand on my shoulder, squeezing, mimicking one of Pops's favored moves. "You ought to call Pops back." His tone is wary like he knows it's none of his business.

I almost roll my eyes. "Is this why you're here? You're Pops's messenger?"

He snorts. "Nonna's, but I've also missed you."

"Then at least buy me dinner." I walk toward the door.

"What the hell happened, anyway?" he asks, talking to my back.

"I just had enough."

"Okay."

I can tell he wants more from me, so I turn around and say, "Listen. This doesn't go farther than you and me, but I plan to marry Christa. Pops said some things about that idea I won't repeat, and I left."

"Ever since you've been gone, he's been ramping up the pressure on me to take over," Max says. "I'm not doing it. He knows it, and . . . Well . . . I haven't seen him this down since Rookie died."

My leaving is in the same sentence as a horse, but it doesn't upset me. Rookie, Pops's quarter horse gelding, was a fine animal. Horses and dogs are better company than humans a lot of the time.

We wait in silence for the hostess to seat us. The place isn't nearly fancy enough to suit Max's typical taste, but the food is good, and I order for both of us.

He won't complain.

"Why are you here?" I ask once the waitress brings our drinks and leaves.

He sips his iced tea, and I can feel him thinking, working up to saying something. I don't know what it is.

Tired of waiting, I intervene. "Whatever's on your mind, say it."

"I don't like how we left things last time we talked."

"About?" I prompt, even though I know he's referring to our conversation about Cody Harris. I want to know which part of the conversation is bothering him. Does he still want to turn himself in? I stare him down, waiting for him to fill me in.

He refolds his napkin and then squares it against the edge of the table, like the control freak I know and love.

"About what?" I ask again, starting to show my irritation.

"The check. I've thought about it a lot, and I still want to send it to Cody and pay off your judgment."

"You're neurotic. You know that?"

"I'm neurotic?" He raises his eyebrows. "What about you? Your knee's shaking so bad the table's moving."

I hurl my hands in the air. "What do you want? Send him the check and what? Ask for forgiveness from the guy who killed our parents? After he drank to the point of excess, deliberately got in his car, and robbed us of people incredibly precious to this family, do you think we should send him a check and tell him it's okay? We're over it?"

"I don't know." A crease lines Max's brow, and his tanned face turns ashen. "I don't. It just doesn't feel right, and I'm not sure how to fix it. I can't live like this."

I look at him and laugh.

He takes a ragged breath. "Don't do that. Don't laugh at me."

"You've got it made, and you can't even see it."

He swallows, his Adam's apple bobs, and he leans toward me. His voice is barely above a whisper. "I can't even look at myself in the mirror. You have no fucking idea what it's like to be me, knowing I ruined your life."

He looks at me long and hard, and the tension in my insides twists like something is broken below my collarbone. I push past the tightness in my chest and say, "Give me half the money, and we're square. Like I said, the past is the past. I'll never bring it up again."

"I brought your check." Max pulls out his wallet and retrieves a slip of paper from inside. He slides it toward me on the dingy blue Formica table.

"I knew you'd do the right thing." I flip it open and read the amount, $250,000. I smile. Because, holy shit, we can pay off Christa's loans. Maybe move or buy a house. It's like we just won the lottery.

Seeing the waitress approach with our plates, I fold the check and slip it into my wallet.

"What are you going to do with your half?" I ask once she's gone.

"What are you going to do?"

It's a typical younger brother move, but I evade and say, "You should finish your dining room."

"I thought about that, but I haven't decided yet."

"Tell me you're not still considering sending the money to Cody."

Max lifts one hand in a silent, *I don't know.*

"You're starting to piss me off. Let's talk this through. Do you want to send him a check and tell him it's okay?"

"He can't walk."

"Boo-fucking-hoo."

Max shakes his head, looking flustered. "Let's just eat, okay?"

I try to focus on the food for a few minutes, shoveling bites into my mouth, but they're tasteless. My appetite is gone.

I put down my fork and wait for Max to meet my gaze, then say, "I hate that you're so nutted up over this."

"Me too."

"So . . . Listen, if you want to, give Cody your share. I won't say a word about it, but think about Mom. Was she afraid in the truck after he ran them off the road? Imagine Dad unable to respond beside her as the truck catches on fire. Think about that, then tell me if you wouldn't rather have a dining room for Sterling's."

"Yeah," he says. "I know. I do think about it. Not exactly the way you described, but I've had similar thoughts."

Neither of us says another word until after he's paid the check. In the truck, all the way back, we pretend to listen to the ag weather report.

It isn't until he's stopped beside my truck that Max says, "I know the grandparents are annoying sometimes, but Nonna's upset with Pops. She would help you if you'd come back." When I don't respond, he says, "Pops is sick." He drops that bomb and looks at me, and the message is clear as a summer blue sky, *Are you coming home?*

"How sick?" I ask, wondering if the old man's finally going to die.

"There's a doctor living at the ranch."

# CHAPTER 27

CHRISTA

When Carter gets home from his visit with Max, he sits on the bed, making me tilt forward as I type on my laptop to review a new customer's account profile.

Stress creases his tense brow. My fingers freeze over the keys, then I reach my finger up to smooth the wrinkles away.

"There's something we have to talk about," he says.

"Max's visit," I reply. I can practically hear his mind work and understand quite a bit about him just by how he holds his chin and sets his sexy lips.

"Yeah, so he gave me a check for $250,000. I was hoping to pay off your loans."

I know he wants me to be thrilled. Part of me wants to be, but the bigger part of me needs to understand what's going on. "Backup, please, and explain why he gave you this check."

Carter does, explaining the why of Max getting $500,000 from their grandparents and deciding to give Carter half.

"If it's up to me, he'll use his half to finish his restaurant," Carter says, and I understand his position. He resents that he's been court-ordered to pay the restitution, and part of him is probably still floored that his grandparents gave Max so much while they've given Carter little more than a hard time.

"What do you want to do with your half?" I ask.

"I'd like to pay off your loans and buy you a newer truck, so I don't have to worry about you. That would still leave us enough to maybe buy a house of our own or save it or . . ." He must see something in my expression to make him stop because he does, then says, "I want to know what you think. What do you want to do with the rest?"

"With the rest?" I ask, because I'm not fully on board with the first part. "You can't spend this money on me. I won't let you."

"This is *us*, right?" he asks. "Because that's how we've been looking at things. For a while now, you've been doing more for us than I have, and I'm not going to spend the money at all if the way we do it doesn't seem right to you. I won't even deposit the check."

His words are so adamant that I can't argue. So, I agree. "We'll figure it out and decide what makes the most sense."

"There's more, though," Carter says, pausing until I meet his gaze, then saying, "Max also told me Pops is sick. There's a doctor living full-time at the ranch. He and Nonna want me to come home. That's why Max was here. To convince me."

"If you don't want to go back, we stay in Laramie," he adds. "We go where it makes sense for us to be. This comes first." He points between the two of us.

"I want to go back," I say because it's true. Laramie is fine, but it's not home. I miss family and friends, but I realize it might be harder for him and so I soften my reaction. "If you want to, that is. If you want to make up with them or try to figure this out, I'm on board. Whatever it takes. If you don't,

I'm okay with that too. Whatever we do, we're in this together."

And that's how it will always be between us as we make our way through life. We can count on each other through every hard and beautiful thing that comes our way.

"Thank you." He leans forward, kissing me softly. "I want to go back."

He picks up his guitar from the stand on his side of the bed and gives it a few test strums. Then he starts to play a tune that's a little heartbreaking. Slow reverberating notes, unbearably lonely. Eventually, he adds something more to the chords, creating sounds that are more than sad and eventually building to a faster pace that seems hopeful. His ability to freely express his emotions with only a guitar is mesmerizing and being allowed to watch is like having a window into his soul, a wonderful gift.

It's become our normal for him to sing and play sometimes, but every time he does, it amazes me how many talents he has and how little most people know about them.

I'm still stunned by how good he is at singing and how unbelievable it is that he wants to sing to me. A chill runs down my spine. I look up at him then set the laptop aside. I lay back on the bed and let my head sink into the pillow as the song speaks to my body with such emotional depth that it's hard to explain. There are no words, but this form of communication works with us.

I keep my eyes closed, wanting to focus entirely on the sounds. He moves from freestyle guitar to playing and singing one of my favorite Johnny Cash songs: "Ring of Fire." All-consuming love.

The final note lingers in the air.

He moves toward me and makes the mattress shift. I open my eyes.

And I see the ring, a simple solitaire cushioned in a velvet box, out of place in his masculine fingers. A flurry of butterflies takes flight in my stomach, making me sit forward and focus entirely on him. So much emotion courses between us without words—fear, comfort, love.

"There's something we need to talk about," he says.

"Yeah," I reply, breathy. "What is it?"

"I didn't intend to ask this question the way I'm going to do it. Truth is I've had this ring for a while and I couldn't decide how to ask, and I've been thinking of the park or the mountains or some other place, but it seems like none of what I've planned has turned out exactly the way I'd hoped, and I don't care. I don't want to wait. I want to dedicate the rest of my life to you and the family we've talked about forming. I love you, Christa Blackburn, with everything I am and everything I have. Will you do me the honor and become my wife?"

My throat is choked with so much love it's impossible to breathe. I barely manage to whisper, "Yes."

He slides the engagement ring on my left hand. I still can't believe Carter wants to get married. I gaze at the ring on my finger, amazed he's done this: Picked out a beautiful white gold and diamond ring, figured out the right size, and proposed. Everything else he's saying is further shifting our view of the world. His eyes light up and I can see our whole future unfolding. He smiles and his sexy mouth is so close.

I finally find my words and say, "I love you, Carter, so much." Then I bring my lips to his.

He pulls away from me. "Say that again."

"I love you?" I crook my eyebrow and smile, because I love him so much that sometimes it does feel a little like we're dancing close to something that could burn us down.

He shakes his head. "The other thing you said."

"Yes?"

He whoops and picks me up off the bed, cradling me close to his chest and spinning us around, then he kisses me and it's both perfect and too much for me—just like I've realized love should be. Our shared love stretches me and helps me have a fuller life, while his love for me makes sure I'll never risk walking over that ledge where I love someone more than they love me. With Carter, I don't think it's possible. I never imagined anyone could be so loving, much less that someone so extraordinary would love me so much.

# CHAPTER 28

## CARTER

I SIT beside Pops in the great room. The TV is set to the weather on mute. He's on the couch, propped up against the arm, wheezing out half-snores. A hospital bed has been moved in, positioned so he can see the TV and the ranch, plus keep tabs on everything going on. He doesn't want to be in bed, even if he's having trouble getting around.

Nonna says he's been like this since his stroke three weeks ago.

They've taken his driver's license, and he's having to use a walker to get around. According to Nonna, he's hardly left the house, and his personality has changed. He's mellowed. I don't expect it to last after he starts in on me. She made it sound like the change might be good for our relationship. I think she's just trying to get me to give him a chance, which I intend to do, regardless.

This is my opportunity to say whatever needs to be said and possibly find a new way forward.

I lean back, crossing my ankle over my knee, relaxed, nonchalant, pretending I'm not worried about what will happen when he wakes.

Even asleep and in a diminished physical state, Pops has an ominous energy, making it hard to let my gaze rest on him for too long. I force myself to study him, trying not to see him as hateful. His face seems complicated, with weathered planes carved out of granite. Even his snores carry a hint of menace.

My mind goes to our last conversation. I knew Pops would say I was being rash. Even though my decision to marry Christa was fast, it was right. Just like his decision to marry Nonna was right. He didn't exactly take his time proposing. Nonna's always been a bit romantic regarding Pops, but she says she knew they would get married within the first two weeks.

Pops and I are more alike than we want to admit.

He was right, too, that I needed to work for what I wanted to feel I'd earned it.

Sitting before him, now, I feel different, less afraid and dependent.

His words echo through me the way they did when he spoke them. *Once you've got your shit together, are off probation, living on your own, and have proved you've got your head out of your ass for a few years, you can think about getting married. In the meantime, you'll let Christa Blackburn move on with her life.*

That advice could have been better.

Muted voices travel into the room from the kitchen. Nonna talking to Kay as she comes in from the garden.

I'm mildly annoyed every time I think of Pops's need to control things, but most families have issues communicating with loved ones who are judgmental and overbearing.

I'm here because I care about my family.

It's about protecting what mattered to Dad and the future of the children Max and I may one day have.

Still, I'm not sure what I will say.

I don't want to argue with Pops.

I also don't plan on apologizing.

So I exhale slowly, try not to let my knee shake, and tell myself there has to be a way forward that doesn't include telling him how I feel.

Pops begins to speak, making me realize he may have been awake for a while. "I've been meaning to say some things." His voice is low and grave, sounding frail.

I lean over my knees and wait for him to say more. He's going to use this as a chance to lecture. With each passing second, my pulse begins to pick up pace.

I can already hear what he will say; some iteration of *you're not enough, you'll never be enough.* Instead, he says, "You've always been good at ranching."

"I never expected to hear you say that." My voice portrays a little of my shock. Burning starts behind my eyes, and I blink.

He's still not looking at me but says, "We don't agree often, but there's never been a debate in some areas. We have never disagreed."

It seems far-fetched. He may list them. I wait.

He spears me with gray eyes that match mine and offers a small smile. "You're the obvious choice to take over the ranch."

What he's saying is too good to be true. Nonna said he's changed since the stroke. Still, I wait for the *but.*

With an infuriating slowness and particular focus, he says, "I'm not saying you're going to be the one to take it over, but you've always been better suited for it than Max."

"And why won't you let me be the one?"

He sniffs, saying nothing and everything as he finally lifts himself into a sitting position and faces me.

"Because I went to jail," I say it like a statement but feel it like a question.

"Of course not," Pops says.

*Of course not.* "Then why am I, not the one?" My voice

sounds unnaturally high-pitched and whining, and suddenly I think I know the answer. It comes back to me in what he said when we argued. "You think I'm still a kid."

He offers me a small smile, calculating as a fox waiting on chickens to lay, but he says nothing.

"Well, I'm not. I've been making my way for a while now, and I think you know that."

He nods. "We need to talk about the company you're starting."

"The . . . what?" This conversation is getting strange. Maybe he is out of his mind. "What company?"

"The land you're hoping to purchase with Abner," he says it like a question. His tone is as confusing as my response.

It takes a painstaking effort to make my face impassive as fear knocks against my breastbone. "Oh, of course. I didn't realize you knew about that."

His eyebrows are as animated as ever, pulling into a sullen line, making me believe he might be around for quite a while. Maybe coming back was a mistake.

"Did you think we wouldn't make the connection?" he grumps.

My knee shakes, and I lean my elbow on it to make it stop. "I . . . I figured you'd realize it." Thinking as I speak, I change tact and channel my inner Christa, having spent months talking to her about business stuff. "I thought you'd even be proud of me when you found out, maybe even pleased I was taking the initiative and finding an investor."

Overstatement of the century based on Pops's Jack Nicholson eyebrows.

Still, I'm unwilling to pretend he's done nothing wrong. "We're going to implement some of my plans over there. With you sick, Leland needing a little more assistance than he used to, and Nonna getting older, it makes sense for us to be close."

"It makes sense." Pops's eyebrows droop as his voice lowers.

"We would have given that land to you if you'd come to us with a plan." His voice sounds heartbreakingly sad.

Why couldn't he have just told me that?

Maybe this is why he's been calling.

I sit across from him silently as he rests against the cushion, then lowers himself back to the pillow and drifts into a fitful rasping snore.

I'm unsure how long passes, but the TV has moved on to a documentary about historic flooding.

Things may be better.

I'm pleased with the change in our relationship for about a minute before I feel like crying for no reason.

# CHAPTER 29

CARTER

The 102nd Annual Whiskey Mile Frontier Days & Rodeo has been going on for three days.

I grin at my bride across the arena and blow a kiss, waiting for her to shift her flowers so she can grab my kiss from the air and bring it to her heart. I catch the one she sends back as Max comes up beside me with Lady, Jake, and Baby. Below me, Duke hoofs the soft arena and snorts his eagerness.

I echo his need for action, with nerves tightening my hand on the reins, but it's not quite our turn. Gently, I pull him back, letting him know we must wait. I glance across the arena at Christa, her mom, and Leland by her side, with Skyler, Emily, and Colt nearby.

For every man, there exists one woman who can hold him for a lifetime, and for me, she is Christa Blackburn, a woman who loosens my knots with her intensity and love.

We might have married before now, but we wanted things settled with Pops's health and to have everyone here.

Fourteen months after Christa and I came home from Laramie, Pops is in a wheelchair recovering from a second stroke, but he's beside Nonna in their box seat with a few home-steaders—we still don't see eye to eye, but he knows I'll act on my beliefs, and that's changed things between us. I'm back working on the ranch. They've built us a house. Even as I worry about what will eventually come from my ill-advised deal with Abner, all things combined make me hopeful for a better future.

Jake's health is steady enough to attend the rodeo and be part of our show. His quest to be a cowboy brought me a chance with Christa, and it seemed right to have him here.

I might have wanted to marry Christa on my next breath, but sealing our love this way was worth the wait.

The announcer's voice travels over a tinny PA system, "Ladies and gentlemen, help me welcome Jake Foster and his accomplices, the trick-riding Corbett brothers!"

The gate opens, and I step up on the saddle with specialized handles and lined loops for grabbing and securing hands and feet.

In many locales, only professionals are allowed to do shows like what we do here. But Higgins is a small town, where fami-lies show up to watch the guys they know do crazy things.

We should come with a warning sign. *Don't try this at home.*

We are by no means on the level of professional riders, men like Jake's dad Colt, who've made money at something that's only ever been a hobby for us, but I push the limits of my will and test my body's strength to outdo Max.

That's what I'm thinking as I circle the arena the first time.

I'm alive when Christa's eyes meet mine.

I'm proud when Jake makes Baby follow him toward the center of the arena where he cues her jumps over obstacles.

And I'm loved when Max swings by me in a suicide drag,

hanging sideways from the saddle while flipping me the bird with both hands.

Of course, I take it as a challenge and the show evolves into something more intense, and a little out of control, while the crowd roars. As brothers, this is what we've always done. It feels good to forget the things that changed us and ride like we are young, innocent, and unafraid.

We're both winded by the time Jake makes Baby sit back on her haunches, ending the performance.

The announcer steps in, with a booming, "That's it, folks. Hope you enjoyed the show. Come back next year for more rodeo, or stick around if you want to watch a wedding."

And I'm smiling so wide, I barrel across the arena toward my bride, out the back gates to where I crashed into her booth.

She's astride a spirited but gentle white Arabian mare. Wearing a white dress, a turquoise pendant, and flowers in her hair, she's beautiful.

Pulse racing, I draw Duke into a slow walk, stalking toward her. Showing off her sweet legs, a thin fur garter on her thigh, she looks every bit like the Western angel she is.

But when I meet her gaze, I can't help but stare into the hottest glare I've ever encountered. "You could have killed yourself."

And I love how much she cares. This protective side of her lets me know she wants me around. I lower the timber of my voice, so she'll know I'm earnest. "I'll be safer next time."

Behind us, her father laughs. His daughter is still the prize he'd die to defend, and I am thankful to have finally earned a chance with Christa, along with a bit of Leland's respect.

Melody stands beside him wearing a white dress. She swats Christa on the thigh. "Go on and marry that boy."

Christa sends her mom a lethal glare, and I love her patience in dealing with her mom, and I love Christa's stubbornness, assuring she will always think for herself. She will need both those things to stick with me, and having her makes me want to be a better man.

She trots off, slowly, and I watch her ride into the arena mesmerized by our history and still awed that she came after me in Laramie when I had nothing to offer.

I'm wondering how I got to be so lucky when Duke lets out a high-pitched whinny, wanting to follow Christa, who's urged her mare into a swift canter.

I give Duke his head. We take off, hopeful and eager, putting on a show that has the crowd roaring all over again as I chase my bride around the arena, galloping by the time Duke catches up, plowing to their side.

Without looking at me, Christa draws the mare to a slow walk, and I'm thinking she's madder than I thought and maybe I've screwed everything up again with my need to show off.

The announcer, a Baptist minister by profession, has come down from the booth and waits for us in the center.

I bring Duke beside Christa, and she grins wide like she's as happy as I am.

Tension eases out of me. "You forgive me for riding crazy?"

She reaches out and runs a hand down my bicep, squeezing it, then lifts one eyebrow. "You're apologizing for that?"

"I mean—"

"No." She shakes her head. "You can't. I worry, but do I want to miss seeing how hot you are?"

I smirk, because I love this shit best of all: the effort, the power, the praise of a crowd.

"I know you love doing it," she says, "and I love you so much."

"I love you too." I lean in and kiss her, earning whoops from a few spectators, making me say, "I just realized I'm not supposed to kiss you yet."

"Well, then," she asks, "what are we waiting for?"

We urge the horses toward the minister, enjoying the moment.

My eyes drift to her legs, the ultra-thin strip of white fur on her thigh.

Catching me staring, she grins. "What?"

"I still want to see that fur bikini." I send her a wicked grin.

Wordlessly, she answers, shifting her seat and showing me a little more leg and a tiny white strap before she readjusts her skirt.

And a whole new fantasy blooms in my mind.

As I promise to love her forever, we recite vows inspired by our song, Johnny Cash's "'Cause I Love You." I know I can count on Christa to go all the way with me. To love me and trust me and keep me entertained.

And when I kiss my wife, I know our love will last.

***

Did you enjoy reading this book?

If so, I'd appreciate it very much if you wrote an honest review. It doesn't have to be anything long and complicated. Just a simple statement that you liked the book and what you found interesting about it—or for that matter, why you didn't like the book.

Anywhere you post the review will help spread the word about this book's release. But I will appreciate an Amazon review. Here's the direct link: http://www.Amazon.com/review/create-review?&asin=B0CDQVK7W4

Please help me fulfill my dream. A review goes a long way to help sell books.

Thanks! I really appreciate it!

Sage

*Read on for a sneak peek of LEGACIES, West Creek Ranch Book 2, where Max is sidelined by a big city/big money daddy's girl whose father has it out for the Corbetts.*

## CHAPTER 1

### ELLEN

Father's name flashes across my car's heads-up display, causing words like acid drainage and toxic hellhole to burden my conscience.

The sour taste that's lingered in my belly rises into my mouth.

In the passenger seat, my friend Babs raises her perfectly plucked eyebrows then fiddles with the radio from the passenger seat until an episode of our favorite gastronomy podcast plays. The host's excited chatter about being a healthier, happier foodie through meditation sends a slippery knot churning inside me.

Yesterday, I quit working for my father's Manhattan-based mining conglomerate, and this trip to Virginia, paying tribute to Mom's outdoor oven, will help me decide if saving her bakery is worth letting Father disown me like he's threatened to do if I don't come back to work tomorrow.

Babs pulls my focus back to the moment. "When my parents cleaned out their basement, I ended up with a U-Haul of stuff."

I stroke the soft leather steering wheel. "It's not like I have anywhere to put an outdoor oven."

"I know, but this is *the* oven. The one you tell me about every time you eat good bread. The oven that puts that funny look on your face and makes you talk about starting a bakery."

A closed gate cuts off access to a long driveway, and I park the car. Tree limbs litter the ground, and dense foliage chokes ancient trees. The land is beyond overgrown. It's abandoned.

"What the hell?" I say, or try to say, because only a whisper comes from my mouth. Father is meticulous about maintaining his investments.

"You okay?" Babs puts a hand on my shoulder.

"Fine. Promise. I'm—"

Before I get more words out, her phone rings.

I step out of the car, leaving Babs to finish her call. She's probably talking to a restaurant client about their next marketing campaign, and it's good she's distracted because I can't explain how hurt I am about Father letting Mom's home go like this.

I'll refuse to think of what will happen after this visit. For a few hours, I can imagine what it would have been like if I never went to work for Father. My job wouldn't include forging mining compliance reports.

I lift the wooden gate over pebbles and moss. A plank falls free, and I risk my nails to wedge it back into place, but I'm wearing wobbly heels, the wood is rotten, and the effort feels futile. Like I've come home too late—again. Every aspect of this trip feels wrong. I'm once again going behind Father's back to spend time in Virginia.

I return to the car and settle behind the wheel. Babs shoves her phone into a fuchsia Marni handbag that complements her magenta hair, but her expressive gaze has lost its usual glow.

"Everything okay?" I ask.

Babs's shoulders sink. "My building's being condemned."

I'd ask why, but I've been stuck in her building's elevator more times than I can count. "Can they do that? You have a lease, right?"

She rests her head against the window with a faraway look in her eye. "I don't."

"How have you been living there?"

"Squatting with permission? Anyway, it doesn't matter because I'm moving, and I need a roommate." She pauses and grins at me as if to say, *Hello, roomie.*

Typical Babs. I love her, but it annoys me when she does things like this. I offer a tight smile. "I don't know. Maybe?"

She lifts one shoulder and forces a half-smile.

Awkward silence fills the car with the sound of my tires on gravel as we pass the gate to the farm. I don't want to hurt her feelings, but I've already made enough mistakes. The dream I've had—to reopen the bakery—feels risky. Letting Babs move in might be another colossal error for my future and our friendship.

"Ready to see your old home?" Babs asks.

I nod.

"So why are you driving three miles an hour?"

*Crap.* She's right. I press the throttle. "I'm taking in the scenery. It still has charm. Don't you think?"

A long driveway leads through the hundred-acre farm. Oaks grace the borders. Kudzu vines have encroached even more since I've been here. Everything is shabbier six years later.

Babs says something, but all I can think is that I don't particularly want to work for Father at all. I just want to go back to before Mom died and start again.

"He'll give it to you," Babs says, seemingly out of nowhere, until I realize she's been talking, and I've been too distracted to notice.

"Sorry." I offer an embarrassed smile. "What were you saying?"

"Your dad doesn't have to sell. It's not like he needs the money."

"No." I grip the steering wheel hard and shake my head. "You're right. He doesn't have to sell."

"I bet he'd give it to you."

"I don't think so." I remember Father's words: *I'm getting you out of Virginia. I'm freeing you of fatalistic thinking and destitution that puts good people into early graves.* I keep my gaze fixed on the middle distance, letting the endless length of entwined tree branches blend into a never-ending tunnel.

"He bought you this car you never drive for your birthday."

I get what she means. A G-Class Mercedes is a nice car. So was the Rolls Royce two years ago. I'm grateful, but I didn't ask Father for these gifts or pick them out. Staying on topic, I say, "He hates Virginia. He hated that my mom wanted to live here when he was in New York. He won't let me keep the farm."

Babs doesn't understand my father, but I do. A Virginia folk singer wiping dog shit on Father's silk Isfahan rug wouldn't have earned more of his scorn than I did when I told him I wanted to re-start Mom's bakery. "If he finds out we're here, he will be incandescent. And not in an 'I'm so proud of my daughter the baker, sort of way.'"

"Then why let him dictate? You said you have the money to do this, so what would he do?"

I should tell her about his threat, but I can't handle her rant. "It would cause a fight."

"And you don't want to fight." Babs quirks her lips to one side as she looks at me.

"I don't." I'm not Babs. I can't dye my hair magenta. I smile tightly and embody the polite daughter Mom raised. "I'm not like you."

Babs crosses her arms over her chest. "I won't act like I understand what it was like to grow up with your Dad's parenting brand, but even I can see you love this place."

"Of course, I love it. All my best memories happened here."

*Along with a few of my worst. Like the day I found out my ex-boyfriend Peter was robbing me.* Beyond the tree-lined driveway are luminous green pastures, highlighted by early day sun. Old barns, seeming ready to topple, are the remnants of a beautiful farm past its prime. Babs is right, my life is very privileged, but that privilege comes with responsibility. I can't leave Father's mess. I'll probably go back to Cross Mountain. Pressure builds behind my eyes. *Stop feeling sorry for yourself.*

I swallow hard and weave the car through the last cluster of trees, expecting the house will come into view. Only it doesn't.

Piles of concrete mixed with splintered timbers lay spilled across the ground like a carcass.

There is no house.

My heart pounds into my ears. Distorted sounds become incoherent murmurs. Babs says something, but I can't hear it. I park next to toppled stones of a garden wall, hand-built by my Grandpa Warren, who died when I was nine.

Leaving the driver's seat, I climb over the rubble, skinning my palms and shins against mortar-streaked rocks. I reach what's left of the oven, sink to the ground, and remember sitting in the sunlight, surrounded by butterflies so tame they landed on my finger. The fragrance of Mom's bread mixed with smoke—the lure of the fire's heat in winter. Memories flood me with warmth, even now, amongst the ruin.

I look down at the concrete foundation, and, for one delirious instant, I imagine rebuilding the oven, making my own life. I take a deep breath and remind myself of Father's manipulative side. He wants me to beg. He wants to be the one in control. He knew the farm had been demolished before he mentioned selling it. Maybe he never planned to tell me. Maybe this is why he was so mad when I said I was coming here. I thought the oven was safe.

A choked laugh escapes my lips. It's almost a sob.

"You okay?" Babs gives me a long look and then gazes over

my shoulder. I feel her intensity as she focuses somewhere in the distance as if her life depends on withholding judgment.

I try to nod, but my head feels too heavy for my neck. I stare at her and shrug my emotions off. "I guess."

Babs huffs an exasperated breath before standing. She towers over me. "Bullshit. You're so scared; you're not going to react at all. Your dad tore down your dream oven, and you won't tell him about it?"

She walks a few steps, then swivels to face me and tilts her chin up. "I probably shouldn't say this because you'll spend the next hour defending him, but some parents don't deserve to be loved like you love your dad. You're always saying 'fine' when you should be saying a different f-word."

Her words roll over me. Anticipating this trip, I brought everything to bake Mom's rustic sourdough one last time as tribute. A promise to her that one day soon, I would be happy.

"You should be angry he didn't tell you he'd torn down your home, but instead, you're like, 'whatever.'"

I summon every ounce of the respectful daughter that Mom ingrained in me from birth. "I don't own this place. I couldn't have stopped him."

"He should have told you."

"He didn't have to."

"No. Don't act like he did nothing wrong. While he's busy making you live by his rules, he's not the dad you need him to be. Not that I want to tell you what to do, but a guy like your dad—" She shakes her head. "Doing things his way isn't going to get you anything."

"My mom knew him better than anyone."

"Maybe she was wrong."

"She hardly ever argued with my father."

"That you know of."

And suddenly, the anger building inside me is all pointed at Babs. I spring to my feet and step toward her, my voice hard and hurt. "It must be easy to be blunt when it comes to speaking about someone else's parents, and I might hate my father at times, but he was there while Peter sold photos of me to pay his attorney's fees. He held me when I hurt because the man I loved wasn't real." Hot shame burns my throat as the words leave my lips, but Babs knows what a wreck I was. After years of counseling, I still attract men who want to talk to me about Peter. They promise to be there for me. They see my vulnerability and somehow intuit that I still don't understand how things with Peter happened. "Even this is better than that," I say to Babs. "I don't have any other choice. My father owns this place. If God himself issues a proclamation, Ed Jasper will not sell me this farm."

I gaze around the wreckage. I could cry, but tears don't fix anything.

I brush the dirt off my pants. "Want something to drink? I've got a cooler in the car. We'll walk around and see what there is to see. Then we'll get some lunch."

"You're care-taking me right now?"

"It's better than thinking about *this*." I wave my hand vaguely as if the wreckage of Mom's oven means less than heartbreak.

"You're a classic avoider," she says, "but I'll let you off the hook because I love you."

I wrap my arms around her. Her embrace is warm and reassuring. More than anything else in this moment, the connection of having Babs accept me as I am, is what I need. When we break free of each other, it seems as if this could be surmountable.

We can walk around and see what's left. Maybe I can still bake something, and that memory will be enough to tide me over so I can go back to work for Father and bide my time. I may be able to stop him from dumping toxins into the environment, and I'm the only one who could. His carefully managed shell operations are so solid no one else even knows he's doing it. If any of what he promises is true, one day, I could sit at the head of Cross Mountain, one of the largest mining conglomerates in the country. I could use the money for environmental remediation and philanthropy.

But what if I turn out like him? What if that's my future? How will I ever escape if I go back? How will I live with myself if I keep forging documents? I feel as lonely and lost as I was years before, sitting at Mom's grave after they buried her. Taking a few deep breaths calms my racing heart. Still, my reality feels less stable. No good choice exists.

After taking a refreshment break, we stalk toward a dilapidated barn, moving to what's left on a dust-caked workbench.

My attention stalls on a familiar logo underscored by an address in rural Wyoming. *The Talisman.*

Finding the oven destroyed messed me up—big time. Seeing *The Talisman* in a ramshackle barn is like a bucket of cold water to the face.

No wonder this quirky newspaper grabbed my attention when I first spied the copy in Father's mail. Articles about self-reliance published each month clone Mom's values. The paper's arrival must be a carry-over from the past. A message from heaven. Mom shining hope down on me from the afterlife.

I flip the pages to the ad that's in every issue.

*HOMESTEAD AVAILABLE: Candidate must demonstrate honesty, integrity, and a solid work ethic. To apply, send a brief biography, along with why life on a Wyoming homestead would suit you.*

If I go to Wyoming and learn to live as these people do, it could give me the distance to come back refreshed and capable of making a difference in Father's company. Maybe these principled people can guide me through this, and I can return strong enough to face him.

---

Ready to read more? Order your copy of LEGACIES now!
www.sageevans.com/books
On Amazon: https://a.co/d/ed2etA2

# ACKNOWLEDGMENTS

My husband, Scott, you are the man in my life. I'm grateful and lucky that you're still into me after all these years.

Thank you to Karen Yeter. You have cheered me on for so long and have helped me countless times.

Thank you to my critique partners, Vicki, Maureen, and Leah. You are awesome early readers and helped to shape this story into what it is. Thank you to my sister, Andrea, for always being there. Thanks to Kelly Siskind an awesome author I admire. I am grateful for your help and encouragement. Thanks to my proof-reader Rebecca Allen for your spot on suggestions.

Thank you to Keri-Rae Barnum and New Shelves for helping me turn a manuscript into a book.

And lastly, thank you so much to everyone who reads, reviews, buys, borrows, lends, and posts about my books. You are why I write, and I am infinitely grateful.

# A NOTE ABOUT THE AUTHOR

Sage Evans lives in a tiny Colorado town—so small there is no stoplight. Everyone knows everyone, and if she's not running with her dogs, shoveling snow, or mowing a lawn, she's buried in a book or restoring classic cars and attending hot rod shows with her very own small-town hero hotty.

Sign up for Sage's newsletter at www.sageevans.com for freebies and insider news. And connect with her on Instagram and Facebook (@sageevansromance).

**www.sageevans.com/newsletter**

**Connect with Sage on social media:**
**Facebook** Sage Evans Romance
**Instagram** @sageevansromance

www.ingramcontent.com/pod-product-compliance
Lightning Source LLC
Chambersburg PA
CBHW020151310726

48970CB00006B/2103